FIVE,
SIX,
SEVEN,
NATE!

Also by Tim Federle

Better Nate Than Ever

FIVE,
SIX,
SEVEN,

N*TE!

Tim Federle

SIMON & SCHUSTER BOOKS FOR YOUNG READERS
New York   London   Toronto   Sydney   New Delhi

SIMON & SCHUSTER BOOKS FOR YOUNG READERS
An imprint of Simon & Schuster Children's Publishing Division
1230 Avenue of the Americas, New York, New York 10020

For information about special discounts for bulk purchases,
please contact Simon & Schuster Special Sales at 1-866-506-1949
or business@simonandschuster.com.
The Simon & Schuster Speakers Bureau can bring authors to your live event.
For more information or to book an event, contact
the Simon & Schuster Speakers Bureau at 1-866-248-3049
or visit our website at www.simonspeakers.com.
Book design by Laurent Linn
The text for this book is set in Minister.
Manufactured in the United States of America • 0214 FFG
2 4 6 8 10 9 7 5 3
Library of Congress Cataloging-in-Publication Data
Federle, Tim.
Five, six, seven, Nate! / Tim Federle.
pages cm
Sequel to: Better Nate than ever.
Summary: Now on Broadway as second understudy for E.T., Nate Foster keeps in
close contact with his best friend, Libby, as he faces his nemesis, Jordan Rylance, and
his own insecurities as the cast member with the least training and experience.
ISBN 978-1-4424-4693-9 (hardcover)
ISBN 978-1-4424-4696-0 (eBook)
[1. Musicals—Production and direction—Fiction. 2. Theater—Production and direc-
tion—Fiction. 3. Best friends—Fiction. 4. Friendship—Fiction. 5. Broadway (New
York, N.Y.)—Fiction. 6. New York (N.Y.)—Fiction.] I. Title.
PZ7.F314Fiv 2014
[Fic]—dc23
2012051239

For Cheri

FIVE,
SIX,
SEVEN,
NATE!

The Fun'll Come Out, Tomorrow

In musicals, characters break into song when their emotions get to be too big.

Whereas in *life*, of course, I break into song when my emotions get to be too big. Without getting paid for it, I mean.

"Nate, will you two keep it down *up there? It's almost midnight."*

That's my dad, who has apparently forgotten how exciting my future is about to become. And that people sing and dance in their (incredibly small and poorly decorated) bedrooms when they're excited. Loudly.

"Sorry, Dad!" I shout. But I do this thing where I mouth "I'm not" right before. Gets my best friend laughing, every single time.

"I ought to pack for tomorrow," I say to Libby between huffs and puffs. We have a long-standing Sunday tradition where we belt the entire score of

Godspell until either the neighbors call the cops or I lose my voice. It's our version of church. "I guess I'll need socks? I should pack socks." But this Sunday is different.

"Refocus, Nate," Libby says, dragging me to my own desk. "I've gotta get home soon. And *we* have your first Playbill bio to write."

Cue: hopping, hollering, Dad cranking up "the game" downstairs.

Libby retrieves a stack of beat-up theater programs from her bookbag. "Let's study bios." She has a step-uncle in New York who sends her his Playbills. Can you imagine the luck? This is probably how most normal boys feel when they rip open a pack of baseball cards, suffer through that stick of "gum," and then . . . I dunno. What do boys do with baseball cards? Fan themselves in the stadium heat?

"Flip to the ensemble bios," I say. "We can bypass the stars." We scan the little biographies that actors write about themselves, trying to settle on relevant information I might use to craft my own for *E.T.: The Musical*. "What the heck am I even going to write? I'm allowed fifty whole words to describe a life spent hiding from bullies in bathroom stalls."

"That's a good thing," Libby says, chewing on her lip like she's still hungry. Which you'd know is impossible, if you'd seen the way Libby ate even the *crusts* on our pizza tonight. "Fifty words," she continues, grabbing a pencil sharpener from my *Zorba* mug, "means we get to use a *ton* of adjectives to tell the world where you got your training."

I see where she's going with this. Libby is, among other things, one of the great acting coaches of our time. She's also the only one I know—but come *on*, I'm not even old enough to drive and I'm going to be *on Broadway*. Wowza. Even thinking about it again—

"Nate, you're shaking."

—makes me shake. "I'm just so . . . excited!"

Did you know that "excited" is Latin for "actually-kind-of-nervous-but-in-the-greatest-way-possible"?

"Well *I*, for one, am jealous," Libby says, re-piggy-ing a pigtail. "Not only are you making your Broadway debut—"

(Squealing, jumping, possibly a bedside lamp being broken.)

"—but you *also* get to do your homework online. Not that you participate in class, anyway."

I take this as a compliment.

Knock knock knock, and I practically pee my pants. *"Nathan."* You know when you didn't even know you had to pee until your dad pounds on your door with the kind of strength that's usually reserved for killing a burglar?

"Your mother and you are leaving early," he says from

the hallway, and then lopes away. That's all he has to say. Everything is implied with Dad. . . . *so tell that girl to go home* is implied, as is . . . *and stop squealing, because boys don't squeal.*

"You do know you *look* like him," Libby says, "when you make that face—right?"

(. . . *and don't come back home until you've made us some money.* That's also implied. Though I'm not sure I ever *want* to come back. Not unless they name a local street after me. Nate Foster Way. Heck: Nate Foster *Freeway*.)

"How about this," Libby says, slipping on a purple Converse. Oh God, she really is leaving me soon. "How about you just make it ultracool. The bio? Like, don't even list your junior high theater credits. Just thank people. Important people who have shaped your career. Like . . . peer mentors. Or whatever."

I grin. "Like . . . best friends?"

"Forever," she says, fast.

She kind of wrinkles her nose the way you might see in a cartoon sneeze, fending back unexpected tears. But this is no cartoon. And I'd know, because I've been chased to the edges of cliffs several times after school.

"Who am I going to watch *cartoons* with in New York?"

"We're almost in high school, Nate," she says, switching tones. "We've got to pull it together and quit it with the cartoon business. I've been humoring you, but. Come on." Brilliant move. Nothing averts sobs like insulting somebody.

"Well . . . I should clean out my closet, then, I guess."

Which is technically true but probably won't happen until the very last minute, once my alarm goes off. There's too much to do tonight: get a rough draft of my bio down; brush my dog, Feather, one last time; vomit myself to sleep. While thanking the universe in between heaves.

"Yeah," Libby says, opening her bookbag and heading for my bedroom door. "And I should get home. My mom'll worry that I'm here so late."

"Oh?"

"Yeah," she says, smirking. "What if you put the moves on me or something?"

I'm about as dangerous to a girl as a tube of mascara, but maybe that's the joke.

"Your bookbag's open," I say.

"Good eye."

"Are you giving me a going-away present?"

Libby never lets me go on a journey without supplying all the basics that any idiot would remember to bring. Like donuts, primarily.

"No, Nate. I was sort of hoping *you'd* have something to give *me*."

I scrunch my face.

"Something tangible with a hint of your *essence*, Nate. Like . . . a piece of clothing. Or an old Indian-head nickel. Or something."

I laugh. "When did you get so, like, Eastern medicine?" *Miss Saigon* is one of my favorite shows, so I actually know quite a bit about the Far East.

"Since none of my mom's chemo treatments took hold," Libby says, skin turning a shade of white that could rival unused towels, "and she started looking into alternative therapies. Is when."

Sting. "Oh. I'm sorry. Wow."

"Yeah. I didn't . . . I haven't had the heart to, like, bring the mood down. Since you've been talking non-stop about *E.T.* for two months."

"Oh God, Libster. I'm really—"

"Not that *I* wouldn't. If I were—you know—*you*."

God, I am such an awful person. An awful friend. And selfish. I look myself over. And fat.

"You are *not* fat," Libby says, reading my mind and dropping her bookbag. "So just stop it. They hired you as you are, Natey. Show up the way they hired you." She swigs from a two-liter of Mountain Dew that I hadn't even realized was in her coat. "You think Meryl Streep would lose weight just to please some costume designer?"

I think Meryl Streep would kill herself if the person

she were playing was dead. But I get Libby's point.

"Thank you."

"You're welcome."

"For comparing me to Meryl Streep, I mean."

"Implied."

And at the mere mention of her name, we both burst into Oscar-worthy tears. And sort of fall into each other.

This is it. Good-bye, Jankburg. Hello . . . *everything*.

I hear Dad trudge up the stairs again, but I hold Libby tighter. And before he can *knock knock knock*, I have the guts, boiling beneath seven slices of pizza and a lava of molten Coke, to shout at the top of my everything: "Leave us *alone*, Dad. This is a pivotal moment."

Libby pulls away, her tears stopped quick like a clamped hose, and sniffs back a goob of snot. "Wow," she says. "Where'd that come from?"

"Here," I say, putting her hand on my rumbling stomach.

"Nah," she says, wiping a crystal tear from her pudgy porcelain face and placing her hand on my heart. *"Here."*

From outside my room, my father's feet squeak in the carpet as he turns in his thousand-year-old slippers, stomping away to take it all out on my mom.

And I know exactly what to give Libby as a going-away present.

"What was that for?" she says.

"I don't know. I've never . . . had one."

"Well, you could at least have opened your mouth a little," she says, holding her lips like they're a wounded butterfly.

We both hiccup at the same time.

"If I'd known that was coming, I'd have skipped the last piece of pizza," she says, letting her lips go like they might fly away.

We both can't believe I did that. Kissed someone. Finally.

"I'm . . . I'm going to leave on that note," she says for maybe the millionth time. "Your mom is gonna be pulling the Grand Caravan into the front yard in about five seconds."

But Libby's wrong. I've got longer than five seconds till the next chapter of my life starts—the first one *worth* singing about.

"Yeah."

Heck, I've got five *hours* till my alarm goes off. Maybe I'll even sneak Feather into bed, where he's not allowed for all the obvious mom reasons. Five hours' sleep is five more than Libby and I got on New Year's, and that was only a couple nights ago. Look at us now! Barely yawning.

"I feel like I'm going to fall over," Libby says, her eyes fluttering—like the butterfly forgot which body part it was playing.

"Let's sit on my bed," I say, "and listen to our favorite song." And never say good-bye. "And I'll see you on Skype tomorrow night, from Queens." Assuming my aunt has high-speed Internet. She must. She's under forty.

"You have the headphone splitter?" I say.

"Was *Sweet Smell of Success* robbed of a choreography nomination?"

Libby pulls out her iPod, but we're practically asleep by the time the song even starts. And maybe it's my murky brain fluid talking, but I get the perfect idea for a going-away gift.

"Gimme your bookbag," I murmur, and Libby does, not even opening her eyes.

I drop it in—the green rabbit foot that hangs by my bed. Libby gave it to me as good luck, forever-and-a-half ago. And carrying it to the audition, that fateful New York day—with that flipping green bunny foot scratching a green bunny nail into my pale Natey thigh—look where all that luck landed me.

My heart speeds up again. This is actually happening. Tomorrow night at this time I'll be avoiding muggers in Times Square.

"There's a surprise in there for you," I say, zipping up Libby's bookbag.

"Good," she says, pulling the earphone from my head, "I was hoping you'd settle on the rabbit foot."

"You peeked?"

"Nah," she says. "Didn't have to."

I guess we both know that the kid with the sick mom could use the rabbit foot more than the kid who's escaping junior high torture.

A light pokes through the slats of my blinds. I sit up straight.

"It's not a burglar, Nate," Libby says, yawning so hard I can hear pepperoni digesting. "The sun's just coming out."

"'Betcher bottom dollar,'" I say. God, I wish there were a boy role in *Annie*.

"Careful, Nate," Libby says, turning a pillow over to find the cool side. "First you kiss me, then you talk about my bottom. People will say we're in love."

"There'd be worse things."

(There'd be worse things than being born a boy who chases girls, believe you me.)

"Broadway's gonna be a piece of cake after middle school," Libby whispers. "You just have to carry our three rules around with you like a loaded water gun."

"You bet."

"One?" Libby says. She's the only thirteen-year-old who gives pop quizzes.

"We text each other so often that our phones break."

"Right. Two?"

"Sing as loud as possible, as often as possible, in as many rehearsals as possible."

"—in order to get more solos. And possibly replace the lead. That's right. And three?"

"I steer clear of Jordan Rylance—*speaking* of leads—at all costs."

"The little *Via Galactica*."

"Watch your mouth," I say, chuckling at our always hilarious routine: substituting Broadway show flops for swearwords. (*Via Galactica* played for, like, four days in 1972, at the Uris Theater. It is only a quasi-flop because it's the same theater where *Wicked* plays, now. So it's automatically sacred, in a way.)

"I'm telling you, Nate, avoid Jordan Rylance. Pretend from day one that he's contagious with something."

Libby knows Jordan—the (luckiest) kid (ever) cast as Elliott in *E.T.*—from before, when she used to go to the fancy performing arts school with him across town. Before her mom got sick. Before Libby had to move to Jankburg, and meet me, and reroute my drifting destiny like a gust of glittery wind.

"What are the odds of two boys from the same hometown getting cast in the same Broadway production?" I say, and I really wonder it. I wonder it deep into my mattress, which I feel like I'm falling into, now.

"What are the odds we'll even fall asleep tonight?" Libby says, or I think she does.

We're too busy falling asleep. One last time.

Legs intertwined. *Wicked* on repeat. Bags not packed.

Before the second adventure of my only lifetime starts—with no lucky rabbit foot in sight.

Blurp

It's a tough thing to know what to bring for your first rehearsal, you know? You probably don't, actually.

"Are you sure I don't need, like, a bunch of pens?"

I'm talking to Aunt Heidi, my guardian till Mom sorts out her job back home. A guardian is like a bodyguard who wears jeggings.

"I'm *sure*, Nate," Aunt Heidi shouts. "You don't need a pen."

We're dodging rush hour commuters.

"But pens are so *fun*."

Basically the most fun part about the first day of anything is buying all the supplies. Plus, kids love it when you loan them pens. Easy way to make friends. New friends.

All new friends.

"You have to use a *pencil* to write stuff in your script," Heidi calls over the tourists, "in case you have to erase everything because they, you know, change the blocking. Or cut your role entirely." Spoken like a true former actress.

Aunt Heidi grabs me by my coat and pulls me out of a light pole's path. I hadn't even noticed it. In New York City, everything is like a 3-D movie—with the unfortunate detail that you haven't read the script and don't know if it'll all end up happily ever after.

"I hate pencils," I say. "Pencils and I have a dangerous relationship." If you don't know what a lead tattoo is, do *not* look at my thumb.

"We're here!" Aunt Heidi always knows shortcuts. Feels like we left her place in Queens about ten minutes ago. "It's your first rehearsal, buddy!" I make a mental map that we're just across from a (gorgeous) Applebee's, and right next door to the infamous Chevys where my audition adventure once got fueled on free salsa. But I don't mention either of these restaurants, since Aunt Heidi knows her way around the upscale dining industry. I wouldn't want to, you know, brag about how the competition offers free refills and stuff. And crayons.

Maybe I should have packed *crayons*.

"Nate!" She's squatting, looking me over. "We've *arrived*, distractible nephew of mine. Gotta get you upstairs."

From the second we get inside, it's obvious this

building is *nothing* like where I had my audition—a place that was a little broken-down. Here, it's like . . . a museum. Gleaming and pumping with the promise of your whole future, just six stories up.

"There will be professional babysitters and everything up there," Aunt Heidi says, pulling me toward the elevator bank in the lobby and fixing my collar. "So be on your best behavior. Make the Midwest proud."

"You bet, Aunt Heidi." Great. The reminder that I'm the Foster family's only hope at glory. "I'm all set."

"Just make sure to listen to what the director has to say today and record everything in the music rehearsal. And, you know. Have *fun*."

She says the fun part so loudly, I realize I haven't been smiling at all. That my lips are totally cracked over. And I haven't even thought to put any peppermint lip balm on today, so you *know* I'm in a daze.

"Young man?"

We flip to the security guard. Always a security guard in this wonderful town.

"Are you with a show?"

Heidi gives me a smile and pushes me toward him. "He sure is."

"Which one?"

"Which ones are rehearsing here?" I say. Might as well know whose elbows I'll be looking up at and almost rubbing in the elevator.

He shows me his clipboard: *Desperado, the Country Opera*; *Stroman: Just Call Me Stro*; and—whee!!—*E.T.: The Musical*.

"That's it!" I yelp. "*E.T.*'s the one." I can feel myself beaming. I am the sun.

"Okay then," he says, nudging a sign-in sheet across the desk. "Your name should be on here."

And there it is. *Nathan Foster*. Unbelievable. This is really it. And if having my name on the party invite list wasn't enough, the guy hands me a badge (a laminated badge!) with an awesome silver chain. A billion years ago, I used to wear a silver cross, but this is way cooler. And more like my true religion.

"Smile, Natey!" Aunt Heidi says, and when I turn around she's snapping my picture with her camera phone.

"Lemme see, lemme see," I say, following her back to the elevator.

"I'll send this to your mom."

"Mom checks her e-mail once a lifetime, Aunt Heidi."

"That's true," she says, fiddling with the screen. Maybe she has an app that'll make me look taller.

"Besides, Libby has to approve all my photos now," I want to say—but we're already whirring away, my thoughts barely keeping up with the elevator. And when the doors part on floor six, we've certainly gotten off at the wrong level: Hordes of folks hug and kiss and whinny like at a family reunion you might see on a TV show. If this is *E.T.*, how could they all know each other already?

"Sign-in is by the main set of doors!" hollers a guy wearing all black. Maybe today is a national day of mourning in New York. *Everyone* is in all black. Or maybe it's traditional to do that in honor of all the folks who didn't get hired for your show.

"This is *E.T.*, right?" Aunt Heidi says to the crowd.

But she didn't even need to, because that's when I see him. *The* him.

Jordan Rylance stands across a shiny corridor, shimmering like a mirage, surrounded by a hazy team of tight-faced, deliriously grinning adults. His Mommy is with him, and I'd recognize her a mile away—wearing that faux-leopard coat, those real-killer eyes. A fancy photographer is kneeling in front of their tableau, documenting the whole clump. "Smile, Jordan!"

That's a true snapshot of Jordan for you. Rich part of town. Rich parents. Rich life.

(Back home, legend has it that his family's even got a koi pond in their backyard. And a carousel. I'm not even kidding. *A koi pond.*)

"Let's get all the children signed in!" the nervous man in all black shouts again. "And we'll start the Meet and Greet inside in two minutes."

More screams erupt. At the level of building-on-fire, at this point.

"I guess I should get running, Natey." Heidi and I exchange an awkward squeeze by the elevator. Jordan's got a camera crew and I've got an aunt who never made it to Broadway herself, even though she wanted it so bad. I feel awful for even thinking that, but there's barely time for guilt, because as I'm placing a check mark next to my name on a bulletin board, a voice squeaks from behind me.

"Do you go to P.P.A.S.?"

I turn to find a doll playing the part of a girl: a purple paisley dress over black tights; shoes so shiny I dare not look at them, for fear I'll get a preview of her underwear hovering above.

"Were you talking to me?" I say.

"Do you go to P.P.A.S.? The Professional Performing Arts School for kids. For professional kids."

Her cheeks are so pink, I actually wonder if she's been seen by a doctor. Then I realize she's in about a foot of makeup. And eyelashes. Fake ones.

"No. No, I don't go to P.A.S."

"P.P.A.S," she says, grabbing a bagel from a table I didn't even realize I was being pushed into. Everything is packed tight in this hallway, especially the noise and energy and intimidating doll girls. "Yeah, I didn't *think* you went to my school." She swipes two cream cheese containers and stuffs them into a skirt pocket.

"Let's get going!" the shouty guy says, opening a pair of double doors and shoveling the clanking group of actors into a rehearsal room.

No. Into a *magical* rehearsal room.

It's hundred-foot ceilings with hundred-foot mirrors, stretching clear across every wall that *isn't* covered by a panoramic window. Allegedly there are families in Pittsburgh whose houses on Mount Washington stare out over our entire little city—but this is even better.

"Hey."

I flip around from the view, like I was caught being . . . myself.

"You can take your jacket off," says a lady around Aunt Heidi's age. "And your bag. And come on over here with the other kiddos."

She leads me over to a throng of youth. My heart goes from sixty to zero, which it always does when I'm forced upon a group of kids in a circle. Though, that said, usually I'm *in* the circle. Getting taunted.

"Introduce yourself," the lady says, taking my coat and breaking up the group. I wish she wouldn't do that. The only thing cool kids hate worse than their party being broken up is their party being broken up by me. But wait. Aren't I . . . *one* of the cool kids now?

"Oh, hi," I say, facing down a lineup of the most beautiful children you've ever seen. Seriously, everyone back home can just give up. The genetic gene pool seems to have found its deep end. "I'm Nate, and—"

"He doesn't go to P.P.A.S."

She's so short, I hadn't even clocked her. But there she is again, smacking away at that bagel.

"Oh," goes a different girl with blonde hair. She, too, is in a fancy skirt and black tights, like it's the uniform. All the kids but me have got a little bit of black on, in fact. I'm the only one in navy blue and red, which I thought would be a nice nod toward America. Broadway is America's greatest gift, according to Libby and anyone with a brain. "Where *do* you go?" the blonde girl says.

"To a school outside of the city," I say. Smart. Nonspecific.

"You mean like New Jersey?" a boy says.

"No."

"You mean like Staten Island?" This, from the blonde.

"I *love* the Staten Island Ferry!" the bagel-chomper squeals.

"Yeah!" I say. "It's where 'Don't Rain on My Parade' was filmed for the movie *Funny Girl*." Finally, an in!

"Oh," they all say. They must be reserving expression and enthusiasm for the show, because they're not giving me any.

"Suuure," the bagel eater says, *"Funny Girl.* Uh-huh. No, *I* love the ferry because I had my head-shots taken on it, at sunset. They've gotten me a lot of work. I mean . . . *you* know *back*lighting!" They all giggle. "Makes you look younger," doll girl says. "Helps for print work."

The girl looks younger than my average pair of Hanes. "Backlighting" must make her look like an infant.

"So . . . what's your name?" I say.

"Genna with a G, but it's pronounced like it's with a J."

"Excellent," I say.

"Did you turn your bio in?" Genna says. But fake-sugar sweetly. Genna is like Diet Pepsi. I prefer real Coke.

"Oh, no, were we supposed to?"

"I just see you holding it," she says—and I guess I am. I worked on it with Aunt Heidi last night and actually feel pretty okay about what I came up with. "If your agent didn't already send in your bio, you should probably hand it in now. Just a thought."

"My agent was being such a *dip* about sending it in for me," the tall blonde girl says, cutting in. "And I'm like: I'm not a writer, Monty; I'm an actress." The children nod, and one touches her back very softly. "Just list my credits. *You* know what I've done, even if I got half the work myself through my *own* connections."

"I hear you," Genna says, swallowing the last hunk of bagel. "I had to produce my own *Web* series before my team would send me in for TV."

"That's awful," the blonde girl says. "Just awful," she goes, but actually that part she just mouths.

"And after that?" Genna says. "It was callback-this and booking-that. And now I can barely get a smoothie in, I'm so overcommitted."

"What shows have *you* done?" the boy says. All the kids face me, the blonde girl tilting her head slightly like I'm an Algebra equation she can't quite crack.

"Oh. I was in a show back home, like a community show that was geared for important social causes."

I don't dare tell them that other than basement performances, I've only understudied the legumes and played the broccoli in *Vegetables: Just Do It*. And that it wasn't even a *community* show; it was at school. The last thing my school has is a sense of community.

"That's special," Genna says, flipping her head away and leaving a fine dusting of aerosol in her wake.

"Let's *see*," the boy says, whisking the bio from my hands and grinning at it. "Let's check the credits." It's a million-dollar grin, by the way.

"*Keith*," Genna says, "be nice to the out-of-towner."

But she's up on her tiptoes, trying to read over his shoulder.

"*Nate Foster*," Keith reads, "*Ensemble, understudy E.T.* You're understudying E.T.?"

"Yeah," I say. "That's what they said when they called."

"Wow, that's mad cool."

"Mad cool," the blonde girl says like it's the first time she's ever spoken, slurring the words together.

Wait. This is *good*. These kids aren't understudies, like me. They've got credits but they're just in the chorus!

"I'm understudying Elliott," Keith says.

Okay, forget my theory. Still. We're all in the chorus together. Not every star can be the *biggest* star, or else everything would, like, light on fire.

"Yoo-hoo!" a woman, suddenly clapping, calls out. "Yoo-hoo, everyone!" She's tiny and British but you can tell she's a real boss of a gal. That's how dangerously high her heels are. And she's not young, either.

I rip the bio out of Keith's hands, moments before he discovers my greatest legacy is as a singing vegetable.

"Welcome," the British lady says, "to the first day of rehearsals for *E.T.: The Musical.*"

Mayhem and laughter and shouting: All of it bounces around the room like an inside joke exploded in a microwave.

"Now, listen here," the lady continues. "My name is Nora Von Escrow and I am one of the lead producers."

Panic, whooping, howling.

"Okay, okay, save it. You've got only five weeks until a paying audience, and we can't waste any time."

No laughter or shouting here, but the fright meter creeps up.

"I want to introduce your very important, very *young* director, Dewey Sampson."

A guy who looks about three days older than my brother, Anthony, steps forward. He's got artfully arranged messy hair, and bright blue Vans, and glasses so thick, you could melt down the frames and make a pretty nice set of chairs out of them. "Howdy," he says, which, for some reason, gets applause and hollers. I barely even remember him from my final audition.

"What else has he directed?" I say to Genna. (Libby and I couldn't find his credits on playbill.com.)

"Shh," Genna says through a smile that's pasted on so hard, my own jaw is aching.

"*And*," Ms. Von Escrow continues, "I might as well introduce you to my old pal from *way* back in England—"

"Watch it now," the old pal says.

"—Mr. Garret Charles."

He parts the sea of people—which makes sense,

since he's basically as old as Moses. Garret, the clever and cruel choreographer from the audition, wears a zippered jumpsuit from toe to neck. His female assistant stands by with a cup of tea.

"Get ready," Garret Charles says, his English accent so stiff-lipped he may have just had a stroke. Or Botox? "I hope everyone brought their tap shoes."

"I don't tap!" a woman screams.

"You will," Garret's assistant says.

"Yes, they will, Monica," Garret says. "They will indeed." All he's missing is a white cat and a chair that can spin around. And my head on a platter; I don't tap either. Oh God.

The producer Nora shoves them over and keeps barking. "Traditionally at a Meet and Greet we go around and everyone says their name and birthplace and dreams and all of that nonsense. But I'm from the old school: We get to work. That's what we're paying you for. You can trade names on Facebook."

Hip, this lady. And this is good: The sooner we get to rehearsal, the better our show'll be on opening night. The better our show is? The longer we run— and the more checks I can send home. That's kind of the only reason Mom and Dad let me take the show, anyway.

"So let's hop to it," Garret says, bellowing, "Stage management!" just after.

On cue, a team of helpers begins flipping and setting up tables. (It's official, by the way: They're wearing all black too.)

"So, can we just sit anywhere?" I say to the lady who ruined the cool kid clump by introducing me.

"I'm not sure, let's see what the director says."

But the director doesn't say anything. The director is cowering behind Garret Charles, who whispers into his ear and pushes him toward a chair at the center of the longest table. Stage management passes out stacks of folders at warp speed, and I take a seat next to Genna.

"Okay," Dewey says, swallowing. "Now. So." He's barely audible above the cast's chitchat.

"Listen up!" Garret Charles says, leaning onto his elbows and smacking a hand on the tabletop. A child's folder falls to the floor and Garret Charles sneers at it. Or the child. Hard to tell through the smog of his dialect.

"So yes. Thank you, Garret," Dewey says, adjusting a necktie that isn't even there. "So the plan here, then. The plan."

"The *plan*," Garret Charles says, playing with his jumpsuit zipper. "The plan is that we're going to read the text. And let's put some real verve behind it. We don't want to start out by cutting scenes that were simply the victims of an underenergized reading."

I can't figure out why the dance person is giving all the—you know—*direction*. But Dewey seems completely relieved, nodding like I do when Libby offers to take the soprano line in "Hard Knock Life." Tougher time hitting those notes recently.

"You'll pardon *us*, Nora," Garret says. The producer perks up in her seat. "But we are indeed *going* to do a few introductions, so the chorus actors know which small parts to read."

"Maybe get out your pencils, then?" Dewey offers.

"Good, Dewey," Garret says, barely turning to him.

We all grab for our supplies, and there's enough distraction that Genna whispers to me: "Video games."

"Not right now, for God's sake," I say. "We're in rehearsal."

"No. *Dewey*. The director? You were asking. He directs video games. This is his first, like, *stage* thing."

"Oh, wow. Is that unusual?"

"Well, he directed *Final Sludgequest 4: Monsoon's Death Mask* for Wii," she says, chipper as a prize ribbon pig, "and it made forty million dollars the first week it was released, so—"

"Forty-*five* million," Keith says, drumming the tabletop with his fingers, since it looks like he forgot to bring a pencil. Not that I'd tell on him, ever.

"They figured Dewey would get our show a lot of

press," Genna says. "Because of the alien thing."

"Aaaand, we're back," Monica, Garret's assistant, calls out.

"So, like, there are bit parts throughout the show," Dewey says. "Little parts where you're not officially a lead but you have to say the lines."

Garret grimaces. "They understand the concept, Dewey."

"Yeah, right. Of course. Sorry. So, will the following people read the following parts." Dewey tries to make sense of a blank page in front of him. Then, from behind: a rugged, wide-in-a-strong-way guy drops a list in front of Dewey and retreats to the corner.

"Thanks, Calvin. Oh, everyone?" Dewey stands. "This is Calvin, the assistant director. And he's basically an amazing guy. We went to college together and while I was playing ultimate Frisbee, Calvin was breaking swimming records and directing the student underground shows."

Man, Dewey's really come to life now. Like he worships the guy.

"So, anything I say that doesn't make sense, go to Calvin. Calvin literally once rescued me from a burning car. Long story. That scene is in *Final Sludgequest 5*, I'll tell you that."

All the kids let out a roar. I've never even heard of the game before today, but I follow suit and attempt a whoop that's timed to start exactly when everyone else has shut up. A stage manager chooses me to *shush*.

"Hi, gang," Calvin says, waving at everyone—but, I swear to God, pointing right at me.

Of *course* Dewey loves the guy. Calvin's unreal, the adult at the audition who gave me important deodorant advice ("Wear deodorant"). He's my hero.

"Now," Dewey says, "let me list off a bunch of little parts. April, raise your hand."

She does: a beautiful, seventeen-foot-tall woman, with bangs cut so low, she may have been born without eyes.

"April, you're going to be reading the part of the school teacher, in the frog sequence."

"*Ribbit ribbit*," is the best she comes up with, but it earns some nice murmurs.

Dewey continues down his list of names, but my mind keeps looping back to the words *tap* and *dancing*. This is an issue. I don't have tap shoes and barely possess rhythm. Usually my "thing" is just to memorize a song and then sing it the same way every time.

"Jake? Where's Jake?"

Everyone's gotten so quiet that something must be horribly wrong.

"Well, I have a Jake here, who should be reading the part of Alien Number Seven."

"*Nate*," Calvin says, approaching Dewey from the

corner. Running up to him, actually, like he's in a relay and my name is the torch.

"Oh, right. Sorry. *Nate*, not Jake."

Even hearing my name makes me go hot. When my name's called back home, it's to answer a question I never know the answer to.

"Nate," Dewey says, "from now on, you're Alien Seven." Garret Charles grunts. Jordan Rylance smirks into his water bottle. Of *course* he does.

"Okay! Awesome, thanks."

I flip through my script and find it—Alien Seven's one solitary line in the middle of the first act. One solitary *word*.

"Blurp."

"Do you need my highlighter?" Genna says.

I catch sight of her script, already premarked. Bold strips of candy yellow blare out from every page. My God: This living doll is playing *Gertie*. Genna is Elliott's younger sister. *Jordan's* younger sister. She wasn't kidding about those Staten Island Ferry head-shots getting her a lot of jobs.

"Oh, thanks," I say, looking back at my line. At my *Blurp*. "But I don't think I'll be needing a highlighter." I don't think I'll be needing a *microphone*.

"And Asella," Dewey says, finally to the last name on his list. "We'd like you to take Alien Number Eight."

(Alien Number Eight has a page-and-a-half-long

monologue right underneath my *Blurp*, by the way.)

"*Terrific*," Asella says, or at least I think she does. I can barely see where the voice is coming from. "You mean I'm understudying E.T. *and* playing Alien Number Eight, eight shows a week?"

Wait. Wait, wait. Somebody *else* is understudying E.T. too?

"Where's my agent?" Asella shouts.

The room scream-laughs, and suddenly a chair scootches away from the table, and Asella (I presume?) hops to stand on it. But even with all that, she's barely the size of Genna.

Asella is my first midget.

Everyone applauds.

"Thank you, thank you," Asella says, taking a curtsy. "I'm thrilled to have logged twenty-five years in show business to end up playing Alien Number Eight." Big group hoots as she hops to the floor, donning a pair of eyeglasses and turning to the guy next to her. "I'm not even Alien Number *Seven*."

Dewey stammers, laughing with everyone but clearly afraid he's got his first controversy brewing. "Ah, don't take it too hard, Asella," he goes, hands shaking. "Alien Seven could be anyone. We needed somebody with depth and experience for Alien Eight."

"*Depth and experience* always means *old*," Asella says, by now doing a stand-up routine, seated.

But Alien Seven is barely hearing any of this. "Alien Seven could be anyone."

"Let's get reading," Garret says, clearly growing impatient. "I have a number to stage after lunch. And something tells me we're going to need all the time we can manage."

"Did the midget lady just say she was understudying E.T.?" I whisper to Genna.

"I believe *the little person* did," Genna says, consumed with a small mirror. "There's two understudies for every part—"

"Act One," Dewey says, "Scene One."

"—and they only put the *best* one on if the lead is sick," Genna says, sitting up tall and batting those giant eyelashes.

"There's something fishy in these woods," reads a gnarled man from the end of the table. *"And I aim to hook a guppy tonight."*

The other E.T. understudy has been in show business for twenty-five years. My parents haven't even *known* each other for twenty-five years. Not even for twenty. I'm as good as dead.

"What's that noise over there!"

I'm as good as . . . well, Alien Number Seven. Who clears his throat and gets ready to read the heck out of his one word.

And You Thought P.E. Was Bad

The best thing to do when you've got a lot on your mind is to unload it on somebody else.

"Lib, hey. Hope this message goes through."

I'm in the bathroom.

"I'm on our first break."

Hiding.

"Just . . . cooling off from the excitement."

God, she's going to see right through this.

"The morning's highlights: We read through the script and I think I nailed my line. Also—"

Beep. I'm cut off, not even sure if the message goes through. And just as I'm hitting REDIAL, the bathroom door whooshes open.

"Actors, we're back!"

Actors. I ignore it at first, before remembering that *I'm* one of them now.

"Coming!" I shout.

When I return to the studio, all the tables have been cleared away, and the whole cast is standing along the perimeter of the room, their eyes trained on Garret and his assistant, Monica, at the center.

"What's going on?" I say to Keith.

"Nobody can figure it out," he says, checking his iPhone with a sly glance. "But I'm pretty sure they're choreographing steps for us. Or something."

This is my chance. Libby and I have crammed a million ensemble numbers into our recent YouTube studies. If I do well in this rehearsal, maybe I'll get put in the front of a production number. That's what an ensemble star is: somebody the audience is basically forced to look at.

"Let's get this *done*," I say to myself. (This is my brother Anthony's personal motto before polishing off an energy shake or dunking my head in the neighbor's above-ground pool.)

Monica, the dance assistant, improvises a triple turn. She whips around so fast, it's like a barber pole in tights.

"Yes," Garret mutters. "That step would be perfect for the children."

The blonde girl claps very quietly to herself. *Dancers.*

"Okay, are we back from break?" Garret says, turning to any available stage manager.

"Yes, Mr. Charles, they're all yours."

"Delicious," he says, but then he retreats to a chair and allows Monica to take over. God, does *this* guy have a good job.

"Remind me who my tumblers are?" Monica says. Back home a tumbler is what Dad pours his gin into. I haven't even figured out the question by the time every child's hand but mine is raised.

"Round-offs? Back handsprings?" Monica says.

"Back, front, side," Keith says. "Whatever." He switches off his phone and rubs actual sleep from his eyes.

"Me too," says another child.

"Me three," the blonde girl says, grinning wide like she's the first person to have ever thought of this joke in the history of ever.

"Nate?" Monica says, making some kind of fish face. "Nothing, right?"

"Nothing," I say. "Right."

"What about my adults?" Monica says, strolling on two high-heeled dance shoes and modeling a tank top that's so sheer, I can practically tell what she had for breakfast. "Anyone have tricks we didn't explore at the audition?"

"I show up eight times a week and never call out sick," Asella shouts.

"Thank you, 'Sell," Monica says. "Anyone else? Special skills? Fire-eating? Et cetera?"

"That depends," says a short older guy, wearing, I now notice, the exact same tank top as Monica. "Are we on a raked stage or what?"

"Okay, yes," Garret says, springing from his seat. "Let's talk about the set design."

For some reason, this gets the room rabid, with everyone slithering into Garret at the center of the dance floor.

"Traditionally," he says, glaring over at Dewey—who's behind a table, talking with Calvin—"the *director* would have presented the set design at the beginning of the first rehearsal."

Monica's staring at herself in the mirror and begins to quite literally kick a leg past her own head. If she's practicing a move that I'm expected to perform anytime in the next thirty years, I'm going to pack my bags at Aunt Heidi's tonight and then quietly write my resignation letter.

"But in *our* director's world," Garret continues, "we apparently don't begin with basics." He thumps his bald head, and reveals yellowed teeth that almost make me miss the cornfields back home. "Nothing traditional about our approach on this musical, *is there*, Dewey?"

Dewey leaps to his feet. "What's that?" he yells. "Are we on lunch?"

"We've got a half hour till lunch," Calvin says,

calm as ever and practically bordering on Canadian.

"Is there anything you'd like to say about your *set* design, Dewey?" Garret says.

"So, yeah." Dewey shouts from behind the table. "So, whenever we're in Elliott's hometown," he says, licking his lips and pressing his thumbs into the air, like it's a joystick, "the set design will be all mysterious. It's gonna be lit like hecka-dark and hecka-flashy, and for all the Halloween stuff it's going to feel hecka-otherworldly. And when we're on E.T.'s *ship*, it's going to look like a plain 1950s living room. It's going to be totally backward and shed a light on what we perceive as, like, truly *alien*."

"That's gorgeous," says April, the seventeen-foot-tall dancer lady who'll be playing the school teacher. She looks as much like a school teacher as my father does a swimsuit model, but that's Broadway!

"In summary," Dewey says, "it's going to freak people out."

He looks like he's convincing himself, which I recognize as the same expression I've probably got right before "shooting" a "hoop" in gym.

"It's going to *freak* people out," Garret repeats, his beady, nervous eyes thudding from actor to actor like stones being skipped through quicksand. "*This* is what we've got."

"Oh!" Dewey says. "One other thing: You're all going to be hauling around a lot of the smaller set pieces. Like . . . Elliott's bedroom and the desks at school. They'll be these light-up cubes that can be pushed across the stage on wheels." He grins. "Think you can handle that, Jordan?"

"Jordan won't be pushing a thing," Garret says, and Monica places her hand on Jordan's head. (His hair doesn't even move, I swear to you.)

"Thank you, Mr. Garret," Jordan *literally* says.

"Sorry to cut in here," the stage manager says, genuinely looking pained. "But we've only got fifteen minutes till lunch, if you guys want to move along the dance portion of the morning."

"Right-o," Garret says, pulling his drawstringed jumpsuit tight. "Monica is going to lead you all through a few basic tap steps. We're playing with concepts for the finale, and I want to evaluate how much I'll need to drink tonight to calm myself down."

"He doesn't mean tea," I hear Asella say.

"Thank you, Garret," Monica says. "Let's get the kids down front, and anyone who's a bit shorter. Or slower to pick up tap steps."

"Is this for all of us?" says the woman playing Elliott's mother. "We're not *all* tap dancing, right?"

She was great in the read-through this morning. Very motherly in a show biz way. She could *really* turn the crying on and off, and Libby says that is what separates a good actress from a singer who just talks in between songs.

"We're *all* tapping," says Garret. "For many of you, tapping is as alien as it gets—even if it *freaks* you *out*. That is our 'concept,' isn't it, Dewey?"

"Did somebody say my name?" Dewey says.

"Exactly," Garret says, folding his arms so hard, it makes his neck bulge.

"Let's spread out and start with a beginner step," Monica says.

I plant myself firmly in the middle of the pack. Always smarter to blend in at first.

"Nate, it'd be smarter if you came down front," Monica says, "because this will be a challenge."

Never mind.

"Let's imagine that E.T.'s spaceship has just flown away into the sky," Monica says.

"The audience won't even have to imagine it!" Dewey calls out. "There's gonna be a giant LED video screen of a spaceship, playing upper-stage!"

"*Up*stage," Garret corrects, power-walking to the double doors and exiting the room entirely.

"The curtain will drop, just after," Monica continues, slowly, waiting to be interrupted but then barreling on, "and when it rises, you'll all be standing there, in a straight line."

"One other thing!" Dewey says. I see the assistant

director Calvin's face contort, probably wishing Dewey'd just shut up and let Monica talk. "There's also an idea," Dewey says, his hair getting messier just by the way he's pacing, "that everybody will be dressed as Elliott for the bows."

The actors squirm. Keith and I catch each other's eyes and we both crack up a little bit. Nice.

"Five minutes," the stage manager says.

"So," Dewey, says, "it's like: 'Who's who and what's what? Are they aliens? Boys? Is there an alien or a boy inside each of us?'"

The room is completely still.

"The only thing inside of me is doubt," Asella says into her shirt collar. For such a tiny human, her voice can sure carry.

"Let's just concentrate on dance steps for the remaining couple of minutes," Monica says, hiking her dance pants up and smiling at Dewey like she's going to murder him. "We can all hop on our left foot, can't we?"

The entire room does, some with more precision and excitement than others. The blonde girl, for instance, is still about three feet in the air when the rest of us have already landed.

"Great," Monica says, staring at the blonde. "Great, great."

Garret comes back into the room wearing woolly

pants and a turtleneck, his outfit changed for lunch.

"How much have we taught?" he says. "Can I see any of the finale?"

"We've hopped on one foot, Garret."

"And then what?"

"That's it," Monica says, digging a toe into the ground.

"At this rate," Garret says, "we'll be opening *next* February." This is delivered as a joke and lands as a warning.

"And I'm sorry to say," says the lead stage manager, a tall guy with an old-fashioned moustache, "that we're on lunch, folks. So we're going to have to hop on our *right* foot at two o'clock."

Everyone skitters to their bags, checking phones before they even breathe. And just as I'm skimming a text from Libby ("u ok e.t. understudy of mine? ur msg was garbled"), Keith taps me on the shoulder.

"A bunch of us are going to check out the marquee."

"The what?" I say.

"The theater. They're putting up the *E.T.* signs today. And, like, doing a photo shoot with Jordan outside the front. On lunch." This is the kind of thing a well-meaning teacher would force a mean-meaning bully to invite me to, back home. But Keith sounds pretty real here.

"We're grabbing iced coffees and heading over," the blonde girl says. She looks like she's *still* hovering in the air from the legendary hop.

"It's twenty degrees out," I almost say. "You're getting *iced* coffees?" But I'm thrilled to be asked anywhere, so I go, "Sounds awesome."

And as we head out for a lunch of iced coffee and Jordan-spying, Monica calls me over.

"You ready to sweat?" she says.

Wow. Such *attention*! "You bet!"

"No, literally. We gotta get you sweating. So you don't pass out in the middle of the show. Gotta get your cardio polished up."

"Oh, sure. I figured rehearsals would, you know, whip me into, like, spandex shape." Shut up, Nate.

"Well, it'll help. But how about coming in a little early, in the mornings? I'm going to be leading a remedial crash course for some of our . . . beginner dancers. And we'll incorporate some panting into the warm-up."

"Okay." What am I going to say? Sorry, my mornings are booked, speak to my manager? I don't even *have* a manager. Libby's the closest thing to it, and she commanded me to show up exactly how they hired me. Fat lot of good that did me. Literally. "Cool. Who else will be there?"

"Asella. And Herbie."

Herbie is a sixty-year-old chorus boy with a wooden leg. I'm in the Broadway special ed class.

"Party time," I manage to say.

"That's the right attitude," Monica says, patting me. "We'll see you after lunch—and then every morning at nine thirty."

"On the *dot*," Garret says, sneaking up behind her like the ghost he's practically ancient enough to be. "We haven't got a moment to lose."

"Come on, Nate," Keith yells from the door. "We might grab hot chocolates, instead, on the way over."

That's more my speed.

"Hot *tea*," Garret says, loud enough that Genna overhears and giggles. She's scooping out lip balm from one of those little jars and spying on the whole interrogation.

"Hot tea," I say. "You betcha, Mr. Charles."

And though I try to be cool about it, nothing could be hotter than how my cheeks feel right now.

Nothing Ice Cream
Can't Solve

You know how "What did you do over summer break?" is the worst question ever?

"How was your first day of rehearsal—*yesterday*?" Other questions can feel the same way. "I can't believe you didn't call me back last night," Libby says. "I feel like you've been gone forever, already."

I'm staring into Aunt Heidi's computer monitor, which glows a soft blue in the corner of her bedroom. Heidi's cat is circling my feet and cozying up to my knee. Frankly, it's almost a little too exciting.

"Yeah," I say, "I can't believe we missed each other online."

Libby adjusts her laptop monitor. She's got a Häagen-Dazs Cookies & Cream cracked open, hacking at the thing with a spoon and letting a nearby bowl of celery go completely ignored. "Well," she says, swallowing an important Oreo chunk, "*before* you launch into the rehearsal report: I've got news too."

I'm delighted to get off-topic. *E.T.* is all I've been thinking about. A casual observer would almost call me obsessed. "Go for it."

"Well, two things," Libby says, picking up her computer. My stomach lurches; I'm not good with sudden movement or change, which should make tap dancing in the finale a real joy. "First of all, I strung lights from my ceiling." She shows off beautiful red lanterns.

"Gorge," I say.

"I wanted a real *Flower Drum* thing in here." She's quoting our favorite unloved Rodgers & Hammerstein score. It was technically a flop, so technically a swearword, but we're not saints, after all.

"And the second piece of news?" I say.

She sits down with her back to a twin-size mattress placed haphazardly against her wall. "The second thing is: now that James Madison has been expelled from General Thomas—"

"Yes?" Ugh. James Madison, legendary bully.

"—the school has taken on, like, a totally new tone."

"You're kidding."

Something clanks from my aunt's kitchen, and possibly even a glass breaks. Heidi's putting together soup and grilled cheeses for us, but "anything could happen" (Heidi's quote) when she's around a stove.

"No," Libby says, "I wouldn't kid about something as treacherous as school. Like, we had a whole Bully-Free Zone assembly, and . . . I don't know . . . I'm restless since you're gone, Nate, so—"

"It's been less than a week, Libby-dibs. This is only the beginning."

"That's my *point*. I think I'm going to start a theater club at school, or . . . I'm not sure. Something to fill the void while you're away."

I hear a knock at Libby's door, and she gives me the one-minute finger and scurries away.

"You're a liar," I say when she's back. "You were gone at *least* two."

"Ha. Well. Mom and all."

"Oh. God. How is Mom? And all."

"Hanging in. Struggling." Libby takes one of her pigtails out (she's got five, to begin with) and moves to her cushy desk chair. We never use her desk as a desk. It's either a makeup counter or a great place to practice flips onto the spare mattress. This is how I almost broke my already-huge nose.

"I'm sorry, Lib. I was hoping for some good news on your *madre*." (I take Spanish.)

"I have something horrible to admit," Libby says.

"Go ahead." Finally, some controversy that doesn't involve whether I can pick up a dance step.

"You know the scariest thing?" She glances back at her bedroom door, decorated with posters from every show that's toured through Pittsburgh. If we had any money, I'd've gone along with her. "If something happens to my mom . . . if she . . . you know—"

"Yeah." I know.

"—I have to go live with my dad. I literally can't even bear it." Libby takes a genuine big breath and not a Tony Awards big breath. "I'm calling it now: His new wife would be found dead by the end of my first week living in their basement."

I don't mean to laugh. "Sorry. Sorry, sorry, but that's funny."

"If you'd ever met her, you wouldn't think it's funny," Libby says, but she starts to giggle too. "Is it absolutely awful that I sometimes have a vision that my stepmother has disappeared?"

"No. That's not absolutely awful."

"And that her head is found in a nearby county?"

"Okay. That's pretty awful."

Heidi pops her own head in. "Natey, bud, let's get you a little dinner."

"Gotta jet, Lib."

"But you didn't even tell me about *E.T.*, for God's sake!"

She wheels back and props her feet on the desk, revealing a teenier shirt than I'm used to seeing her in. There's the chance it's even a croppy top or whatever—the kind Olivia Newton-John wears at the end of *Grease*—but who can keep up with girls' terms?

"There wasn't *time* to tell you about *E.T.*," I say.

In a flash, I realize I don't even have anything I *want* to share. Not about receiving dead silence after saying, "*Blurp.*" Not about showing up at 9:29 this morning to literally sweat with the oldies. Not about Jordan refusing to make eye contact with me—even *once*—so far.

"Who'd have time to brag about his flawless career, when his best friend is rattling on about her stepmother's future beheading?"

Libby grunts. "Pardon me," she says, swinging her legs down, fast, and getting one eye so superclose to the camera monitor, I scream a little. Aunt Heidi's cat swipes at my leg. "I was trying to get the image of my *own* mother's slow degeneration out of my mind."

I gulp. You know when somebody farts in your strictest teacher's class, and you can't say anything? "Good word," I say, feeling myself fidget. "*Degeneration.*"

"Thanks."

"It's a real word, right?"

"Don't be a *Marilyn*, Nate." (Thirty-four previews on Broadway; seventeen performances; all-out flop about Marilyn Monroe—and frankly, a pretty aggressive name to be calling me.)

"I *wasn't*," I start, and then just: "I'm really sorry. About your mom."

Music from Heidi's living room suddenly fills the apartment. Really loudly. She's making a subtle point. "Nate!" she yodels. A less subtle point. *"Dinner."*

"I've gotta go, Lib."

"Miss you, champ."

"Miss you, scamp."

"Hey—Natey Greaty, tell me one thing."

"Yup?"

"You making us proud?"

I think back to standing outside the theater with the other kids yesterday, forcing down that hot tea— the way everyone who drinks hot tea must have to pretend they like it. On their own quest to fit into their costumes.

"Are you gonna come back a star, buddy boy?" Libby takes a big mouthful of Dazs.

"A star," I say. My God. What if I'm an outcast no matter where I'm cast? "I'll do my best, Lib."

And then I get this high-definition memory of Keith, pointing up to the marquee's giant gold lettering: "That is *mad* cool," he said, gawking with the rest of us. "Man, to be *him*." *And introducing Jordan Rylance* written in giant Nate-height letters across the front of the theater.

Libby's mom coughs so hard that it travels all

the way from outside Libby's room and through the Skype wires, and Libby turns around and squints at the door. "I've gotta go too, Natey. Gonna check on the Momster."

"You bet, Lib. And Lib?"

"Yessir?"

"I may be in the ensemble, but I'm trying to approach it like a star. Trying my hardest."

She gives me a cheesy thumbs-up, but it's nice all the same. "Remember, Natey, there are no small parts."

"Thanks."

"Only small actors with medium stomachs. With large talent. Playing, like, smallish roles."

She shuts the clamshell of her monitor just as Heidi barrels through the door. "Your soup's getting cold," she says, finishing a graham cracker. "And I got the daily schedule e-mailed from your stage managers. Gotta get some sleep, Natey. You guys are staging the opening number tomorrow."

Ladykiller

(Four and a half weeks till first preview)

The studio is transformed. At every new rehearsal, the room is crammed even tighter with giant stand-in set pieces. "Let's get the aliens down front and the townspeople in the back," Monica says, holding a clipboard and a coffee that's taller than I am.

"Do you need me, too?" Mackey says. Mackey is playing E.T. He's a pretty amazing character actor who has appeared in every *Lord of the Rings* movie and is approximately as jaded as Libby. Though he has the excuse to be.

"You can take a ten, Mackey."

"Make it twenty," Garret says, piping up from a chair, his mouth teeming with biscuits. "Take a long break, Mackey, because we're working to establish some general movement vocabulary before we add you in."

The rest of the cast is gathered down front.

"Where's Asella?" Monica says.

A stage manager looks up from a pile of paper-work. "She's across the hall in vocal."

"Oh, right," Monica says, consulting a schedule on the back of her clipboard. "It's like air traffic control on a new musical, right?" Half the room breaks into applause, like all they *do* is new musicals. "So, let's start on the opening sequence," she continues. Every time Monica turns to anyone at all, it's like a poem: her posture a yardstick, her legs two stilts. My mom would kill for Monica's figure. Frankly, my mom would probably kill Monica, if given the chance.

"Yes, yes," Garret says, swallowing the last of his snack and jumping up. "It's our opening sequence. This is *very* tricky. Stage management, could you ask the room to be quiet?"

The entire room is, in fact, quiet. The only people making any noise at all are the stage managers.

"Thank you," Garret says. "What we need is fear, dread, a sense of a world being occupied by outsiders. Yes?"

"Yes," we all say like drones.

"We've got Gertie and Elliott wandering the wood, the aliens hiding behind trees. And we're looking to stage the entire sequence without dialogue. That's the concept right now: movement instead of acting."

"Dance," Monica says, as if helping.

"Yes. Danced, like the opening in *West Side Story*. Which you children are too young to know about."

"It's not called the opening in *West Side Story*, it's called the prologue," I'm desperate to say—but I just nod like every other beagle.

Garret returns to his seat and folds an extravagant sweater around himself. You must get awfully cold when you're the choreographer and don't actually dance any steps.

"So," Monica says, addressing the pianist, "why don't we just play some of the opening theme? We'll loop it. Let's all just improvise, and see if Mr. Charles sees any movement he'd like to build on."

"You're afraid, you lot," Garret says in a weird even tone, like he's channeling somebody genuinely creative. "You're cold and afraid and far away from your home planet. Now . . . *dance*."

The blonde girl—Hollie is her name, I've come to learn, because I've been to her Web site and joined her e-newsletter—immediately begins jumping all over, like she's alone in her bedroom. She swirls and dips, and rather than the other kids being intimidated by it, they all appear inspired.

"*Work*, Miss Hollie," Keith says, *beginning* his improvisational movement by flipping backward and landing on his head. Literally.

I dial back to the audition, the thing that *got* me

this job. Relax, Nate. You deserve to be here. And without over-thinking it, I channel Jerome Robbins, who choreographed not only the prologue to *West Side* but also *Fiddler on the Roof*, a show whose famous knee crawls I demonstrated at the *E.T.* audition. If it worked then, I'll try it again.

"Let's get this *done*," I say.

And I'm off, covering ground, pretending I'm a racecar and not a scared boy.

"Watch it!" somebody yells.

One thing about my famous knee crawls is that sometimes I don't look up when I'm doing them.

"Can we get ice?" I hear Monica shout.

For a second I think she's asking for a condiment, but then everyone's gathered around me. And Genna. And only looking at Genna.

"Are you okay, angel?" Monica says.

(She's staring at Genna. Not me.) (The devil.)

"I'm not . . . sure," Genna says, cradling her knee. I'm feeling this more than seeing it, because I'm right on top of Genna. Not sure how that happened. Also, wow: I'm not familiar with this position in relation to other people. Especially girls.

"Give the kid room!" Mackey shouts from a towering stool in the corner.

Everyone backs up as I roll off Genna, and then a stage manager smacks a blue ice pack down on her knee. Garret Charles walks the perimeter of the actor circle, hands on hips, eyeing me.

"Should we send her to the hospital?" somebody yells.

"That won't be necessary," Garret says, offering Genna his hand.

"Thank you, Mr. Charles," she says, and a few of the adults clap like we're in a stadium. (I've seen this happen a lot, because Anthony has taken down quite a few football players, all of them instantly debilitated. They get actual applause when they finally walk off the field. *If* they walk off the field.)

"We don't need hospital," Garret says, allowing Genna to stand on her own. "We'll call upon an old technique I learned in England in the seventies. I want *everyone* in the room to place their hand on Genna's knee."

Genna's eyes go wide, and I watch as Monica beelines for the mirrors at the periphery of the room, gently biting her lip. Everyone else, though, takes Garret's instruction—every adult, child, little person, and stage manager.

"Get to it," Garret says, "we haven't got a millennium."

In moments, they've got their hands all over Genna, which is kind of weird. This would be illegal in Jankburg.

"You too," Garret says, flashing red eyes at me. Apparently I'm standing outside the human hand-mountain, but I feel like I'm watching the whole thing from above, like a ghost. God, do I wish I were dead right now. "This was *your* doing," Garret continues. "Let it be your undoing, too."

I place my palms on Keith's shoulders, which huff and puff and sweat as he smiles at Genna. "You got this, girl. You got this." He feels warm. Bordering on . . . hot.

"On the count of three," Garret says, "we will all breathe in Genna's injury." If anyone so much as hiccups, we'll all topple over and cause some genuine damage here. "And after we inhale the injury, on the downbeat of count *four*"—dancer folks are nothing if not complicated by numbering everything—"we shall then exhale a new energy into Genna's knee."

People are looking wholesomely to Garret Charles like he's the chief of surgery at Dad's hospital back home. Like he *isn't* a deranged quack.

"One," he says, his voice rising, "two"—and April, the hundred-foot ramp of a dancer, is actually *weeping* —"three."

The whole group breathes so hard, I swear a light flickers from above.

"Hey, kid, how's the knee?" I nearly say, but just then, I see Dewey and Calvin stride into the room from the hallway. We all sigh so loudly that Genna teeters on one foot—and then regains her balance.

"I'm healed!"

"I *love* this," Dewey says, skipping over to Garret. "I don't know what sequence you're working on—"

"They're on the opening number," Calvin says, spying Monica's schedule over her shoulder.

"Fantastic," Dewey says. "Wow. Such an image. An entire glob of people—or are they *aliens?*—gathered around Gertie. *Such* power. Wowza, Garret."

Garret twiddles an imaginary moustache. Come to think of it, he doesn't have eyebrows either. God, I wouldn't be surprised if his own reflection didn't even show up in the mirror.

"I mean," Dewey says, the room frozen around him, "I'm not convinced we need the whole *cast* for this—"

"And some of these folks," Calvin says, "will be *offstage* in a quick-change for the scene just after . . ." Monica cups his ear and begins whispering.

"But regardless," Dewey says, swatting at the air like it's a giant iPad screen, "the important thing is that we just found our *closing* image." Dewey hops up and down like a boy who has to pee. Oh my God, I have to pee. "Listen up, gang. Wow. Listen up."

The stage managers call for anyone hanging out in the hall to join the room.

"The last image of the play," Dewey says, suddenly confident, his blue eyes blazing like the two days a year when Jankburg is cloudless, "I'm calling it now—the closing image of *E.T.: The Musical* will be the entire cast embracing Gertie. *This* image, right here."

Genna bows. April is braiding her hair, still crying. (Sniffling, shoulders shaking, the works.)

"Yes, well," Garret says, clearing his throat. "I'm not—"

"Don't be modest," Dewey says, slapping Garret so hard on the back, his jumpsuit zipper rattles. "You're a genius, Garret."

Something swipes my butt, and for a second I flash back to the school locker room. On those horrifying days when I have to change my shirt for gym, one of the bigger kids usually grabs it from my hand and whips me until the coach breaks it up. (Seconds later, the coach is always fist-bumping the bully on his way out. True.)

"Well, *that* was an unexpected turn of events, wasn't it?" Monica whispers. She's smiling, and then, before I can even stop it, I am too. "Congrats," she says, just as stage management is sending us on another ten-minute break. "Looks like you just helped create the 'closing image.'"

She rolls her eyes but then winks at me.

"You should ask your agent if you can get an assistant director credit." This, in a whisper, from Hollie. "Seriously major, Nate."

"Yeah, big ups," Keith says, heading with her to the door after attempting a cool handshake with me. Total fail, but still.

"You're on a ten, too, Mr. Assistant Director," Monica says.

Genna limps to a chair. I guess only on Broadway can you injure a child and get celebrated. Actually, that's not true; after James Madison gave me a black eye last September, he was elected president of our class.

But no matter: I've just done it. I've become . . . *important* here.

"Nate!" a stage manager says, pulling me away from Monica (and back down to earth). "You okay? I saw that you took a pretty bad spill yourself."

I look down, just in case my leg fell off or something. It didn't. "I'm fine."

"Great," the stage manager says, looking at a list. "Listen. This afternoon, we're going to send you across town with one of the guardians."

"Am I in trouble?" Oh my God, they're going to fingerprint me for taking Genna down. Her dad is a lawyer—I heard her say that.

"No, no. Nothing like that. You've got a mask fitting today. On the East Side. They have to take a mold of your face."

A mask of zits. "Awesome," I manage.

But when I grab my coat and head for the door, something catches me off-guard in the hallway. "What's that sound?" I ask one of the adults. "It's, like . . . unbelievable, in there."

It really is. E.T.'s big song blares out from the tiny music studio. And howling above the piano, a human voice buzzes and whirs like it's being sent through a food processor. But in a good way. An otherworldly way.

"Is Mackey rehearsing?" I stand on my tiptoes but lose balance, hitting my underbite on the metal door handle.

"No," one of the music assistants says. "That's Asella."

"Asella?"

"Yeah. They're teaching her all of the E.T. music. Just so she's ready to go on in the event of a Mackey emergency. You know *Mackey*."

I don't really know Mackey, other than that he smokes a cigar on every break and is already not allowed near the adult female ensemble.

"When are they teaching *me* the E.T. songs?" I say to the assistant.

"Who knows," she says, yawning, sorting through a stack of sheet music. "We're only teaching the primary understudies now. I think the secondary understudies have to sort of get up to speed on their own time."

And my guardian grabs a coat sleeve and pulls me to the elevator. Off to make a mold of two worried eyebrows playing the role of my face.

Masks

(Four and a half weeks till first preview)

The whole way over to the mask fitting, all I can think about is Asella, singing the *Pacific*-freaking *Overtures* out of that song.

"Okay, Nate, we're here," the guardian says, slamming the taxi shut and taking me by the hand. Like I'm six.

We make our way up a rickety elevator that smells like shoes and milk, but then the doors open directly into this incredible cavern, with show posters dotting the walls like stars.

"Hi there!" a voice calls from a distant room. It's like an apartment being played by an apartment in a horror movie, but one that isn't scary. The shelves may be lined with giant stuffed raccoons, all right, but they're all wearing wigs.

"Is Nathan Foster here?" the voice shouts.

"Yes, sir!" I shout back.

"You don't have to shout," says the guardian, who's checking texts on her phone.

I have officially decided to pretend like I don't know her name.

"Be right there," the guy from the back says. "You're a little late."

"There was a little traffic," the nameless guardian mutters, "so we're a little sorry." She's not saying any of this to me, but to her phone. Maybe she's on a video call. Rumor has it iPhones do everything, except appear under my Christmas tree.

"Hi, Nathan." Now the voice has a face—a goateed little head poking out of a tight plaid shirt. He's one of those urban-type guys who's ancient but still wears those cool bowling-like sneakers. I want to be this guy when *I'm* in my forties. "You two can follow me back."

Now that I'm not stuttering my name, which happened the instant I got cast in *E.T.*, I should just tell him I go by *Nate*. But then, maybe *Nathan* ages me up a little. I'm practically fourteen, and maybe this Nate business is best left back home.

"Almost there," he says. "I've lived here forever, so this is one of those million-year-old apartments you can't get anymore, if you weren't born into money." I kind of like how nobody hides anything in New York.

We wind around a corner and push through a

beaded curtain and land in a treasure chest of a room.

"Okay, hop up," he says. I hadn't even clocked the barber chair in the middle of the floor—too busy noticing a bear's head, hanging from the wall, looking entirely ferocious if not for its bright red lipstick.

"We hunt bears back home," I say. "Well, my relatives do. Not me."

The guardian grunts.

"Yeah, I didn't hunt this guy," the nice guy says, admiring the bear. "Just found him at a flea market."

"What's his name?"

"Bernie the Second."

"Oh, cool."

"I'm Bernie the First. By the by. Bernie the Second is everything I wish I could be if I weren't designing wigs and masks."

Whoa. Stuck to a wall? Wearing makeup?

"Ever been fitted for a mask?" Bernie the First says.

"My dad tried to make me play hockey goalie in fourth grade, so I guess then."

"Oh." Bernie the First chuckles and swigs away at a mysterious green juice. "Okay."

"And I went as a Smurf for Halloween, a bunch of times. And, come to think of it, I wore, like, a headpiece thing in a play I did back home."

For *Vegetables: Just Do It*, Libby's mom made me

an entire broccoli hat out of old green pom-poms.

"Got it," Bernie the First says, pulling out a bowl of batter from a refrigerator. "So no, you've never worn this kind of mask. But I like those stories. Those are good stories."

I'm paused on the batter. "Are you making *pancakes*?"

The guardian grunts again. Adults can eat anything, anytime.

"Pancakes?" Bernie says, smiling to himself. "Nah. I wish. This is the putty for your facial mold. We're putting together your Alien Number Eight mask today."

"Alien Number Seven," I say. "Alien Number Eight requires depth and experience, and talent, so I didn't get that part," I almost say, but don't.

"Ah, good you corrected me," he says. "I would have made Alien Number Eight mask look like a *Smurf* if we hadn't caught it in time."

I almost ask Bernie if he's ever known a chorus kid who's gone on to become famous, but instead I just go, "The lighting's really cool in here. It feels like we're on a movie set."

He puts the bowl down and picks a fingernail. "I used to work in movies, actually. Made masks for that crazy Mackey, in fact."

"Cool. He seems really nice."

"Does he?"

He doesn't. He seems rough as an unpaved road back home, but "he seems really nice" is just sort of what you say, right?

"Yeah. He seems nice."

"I guess he's changed, then," Bernie the First says, his goatee turning into the frame for a smirk. "Okay, Nathan, so—how are you with holding your breath?"

"Oh, I'm swell at that, Bernie the First!" I get so excited, the barber chair squeaks. "My older brother tried to drown me a couple times, and I slowly built up a resistance."

Bernie puts the bowl down. "You're an original."

"It's true!" It *is* true.

"*Anyway*, I'm going to slather this junk on your face, and you have to sit totally still and hold your breath and not move a single face muscle. Which is very hard for actors."

"Thank you for calling me an actor, Bernie the First," I say.

He laughs. "You're welcome. Thank you for calling me Bernie the First. I should have that printed on my business card."

"Oh!" I say. "Can I get a business card on the way out?"

"Good Lord," I believe the guardian says.

But Libby says I should be sending handwritten

notes to anyone who's nice to me! As an example: The guardian will not get a handwritten note. Bernie the First *will* get a handwritten note, and so on.

"We'll see," Bernie says. "We should get moving, though." He picks up a note pad. "We've got a big *headliner* coming in after you."

He shows me a long list of my castmates: Genna the Injured was here just before me (no wonder the room smells like lollipops and foundation), and Jordan will be here right after me. The big *headliner*.

"Oh," I say. "Him."

"Ah, do we not like him?" Bernie the First says, leaning my chair back. It's very *Sweeney Todd*, but I'm telling you now: Bernie wouldn't slit my throat in a million years, because he didn't even kill Bernie the Second.

"Nah," I say. "Jordan seems really nice. It's just—"

"Ya know, we don't have to get into it," Bernie the First says. "Let's get your face cleaned up and then we'll get you molded."

He sponges my cheeks down with this witch hazel stuff and my skin gets supercold and then supertight. It's cool because maybe it'll shrink my zits down. The toothpaste Libby told me to smear on my pimples at night isn't really working.

"Okay," Bernie One says, "now for the hold-your-breath-in-the-pool part. I'm going to put all this weird oatmealy stuff on your face. It'll be like nothing you've ever done."

"Neat." I don't want to correct an adult and tell him that Libby and I do oatmeal masks at *least* once a week. He seems like he's having fun, and correcting someone can really bring them down.

"So where are you from?" Bernie says, gooping the goop on.

"A town called Jankburg. In Pennsylvania. Have you heard of Pittsburgh?"

"I have," he says. "And actually, I set you up. Sorry. You shouldn't talk. Need to be still."

"No problem," I say, and then: "Oh, sorry. I shouldn't have talked." And then: "Oh, sorry again."

He laughs and swats my chin with the brush. "Quiet, child," he says— but he proves my point that you can say mean things nicely and not be mean. My dad could learn so much from Bernie the First. As if my dad would ever have a mirror ball hanging from our ceiling, though.

"If you can breathe through the nose slits in the putty, nod your head." Bernie steps back. "And if you can't breathe, can I have your iPod when you die?"

I don't have an iPod but I get his joke. So I nod.

"Good. I'm going to be right back. Don't move. Or steal Bernie the Second."

Bernie the First steps out of the room, so my eyes

flick around. He's got a shelf full of awards—are those *Tony* Awards, I wonder??—but my eyes stop dead on a blender, with red sauce splashed across the glass.

"Ah, you found the place where I grind up children's hands," Bernie says. I hop about a foot out of the chair. "Hold still. Didn't mean to scare you."

He slowly peels the mold away. "Pretty cool, huh?" he says.

I sit up and take it in: the hollowed-out Nate Foster.

"Why do you need a mask of my face?" I say. My cheeks tingle, and the room smells like burned rubber—like when Anthony rips out of the yard in his pickup.

"Because we want to have a mold of your facial structure, so the E.T. mask fits snugly."

"So you're making *me* a mask for E.T. the *character*?" This is a good sign!

"Well, this will double," Bernie says, shaking my fake face. "This will be your Alien Number . . . what was it?"

"Seven. The *Blurp* alien."

"Right. Lucky number seven." I wish. "But you'll also use the same mask for E.T.," Bernie says, writing something down on his notepad. "Same bodysuit, too." He lays the mold across a Styrofoam head.

"Can I touch it?"

"Sure," he says. "Just be careful."

"Can I take a photo of it?" Libby would die.

"No, actually. All sorts of producer rules about that. I could get in trouble. You could get in trouble." He takes another sip of juice. "I'd lose my country house. Blah blah blah."

I take my own hollow head and sit it in my lap. This sounds so pitiful, but it's . . . ugly. Lifeless and brown. When you look at a mirror, you're only seeing a fake reflection, something backward. So sometimes when I'm getting ready before school I can convince myself that maybe my hair isn't as bad as I think, or my skin is clearer. Sometimes I can pretend that maybe my nose is proportionate to my face, or my eyebrows aren't so big. It's just a mirror, I'll say. Sometimes I'll say it out loud. But mirrors can lie to you.

"Pretty nifty, huh?" Bernie says, putting the batter away.

But when you're looking at your own face, at this topographic map of your own bumpy nose, there's no denying it: Straight on, I look pretty lame.

"I'm early!" I hear.

A bumpless, proportionate nose pops through the beaded curtain of Bernie's studio. Jordan. With eyebrows that are practically the same color as his flawless snowy skin.

"Sorry to barge in, but I just couldn't wait to meet you, Mr. Billings-Sapper."

Bernard Billings-Sapper! Of course! The Tony-winning wig designer of every hit show in the last four seasons. I didn't even shake his hand. Libby'd have recognized him by the goatee alone and staged a fainting scene.

"Aw, thank you, Jordan," Bernie Billings-Sapper the First (and only) says. "I'm just finishing up with one of your co-stars."

Jordan looks at me. "You mean *Nate*?"

"Oh, do you go by Nate, Nate?" Bernie says.

"Sometimes," I say, handing my head back to Bernie. "But people have all sorts of nicknames for me."

"Come on, Nathan," the guardian says. "We've gotta get you back to rehearsal. And I hope you packed your tap shoes today." I pop out of the chair.

"Great to meet you, Nate," Bernie says. I grab my bookbag and reach for his hand. "Oh, you don't want to do that. My hands are all sticky."

"You kidding?" Jordan says, now striding forth and (*honestly*) patting Bernie on the back. "Those hands have held a Tony Award."

"Four, actually," I say.

"Kids, kids," Bernie says, chuckling. "Stop looking through my shelves when I'm not here."

"I didn't have to look at your shelves," I say. "I know Tony stats like my dad knows the Steelers' starting lineup."

"Oh, Nate, I almost forgot," Bernie says, handing

me a slip of paper. "The last kid left this note for you. But I'm not supposed to say who it's from."

Jordan hops up on the high chair, and laughs. "God, this thing is so warm. What did you do in it, Nate? Run a mile?"

"I don't run miles," I say, glaring at him with fire-eyes. "I *walk*."

I go for a dramatic exit, whapping my big fat nose into the thin beaded curtain. Bernie calls out, "Watch the curtain," and Jordan goes, "Too late," just as the guardian and I hit the hallway.

"Was that fun?" she says, still looking at her phone. Typical adult.

"Yeah, sure," I say, peeling remaining threads of dried mask from my face. I wish I could stay around long enough to steal Jordan's mask. That's a kid anyone would want to look like.

We board the elevator and I pull out my phone to text Libby: "u were right. jordan rylance is such a bad word that i can't even think of a musical flop big enough to call him."

"Whatcha got there?" the guardian goes.

"My phone," I say back, but not in a nice way. They say you always turn into your parents!

"No. The other hand. I know what a phone looks like."

The slip of paper, from the anonymous kid.

wanna know a secret? i'm scared too, and i think your doing a really good job in rehearsal . . . when your not running into people ☺

"Um," I say. "It's . . . it's just a note I made for myself. About picking up apples for my Aunt Heidi on the way home tonight." I am never more specific than when lying.

But it's not a note from myself.

It's a note from the last kid who was here for a mask. Genna. Who wanted to remain anonymous. Who didn't know I'd see Bernie's mask-making schedule on his notepad.

"My aunt loves apples," I murmur.

Genna, who doesn't even know how to use the proper form of *your*, but is the same age as me and starring in a Broadway musical. With a limp.

Genna, who doesn't even know she just made my day. My *week*.

"'merrily we roll along' is the flop ur looking for," Libby texts back. "jordan rylance is a total 'merrily.'"

(1981; played sixty-eight performances at the Alvin Theater. A big flop with a famous song: "Old Friends," all about meeting up again with the only person who ever really understood you.)

"Wow," the guardian says, for the first time sounding like an actual concerned person with actual feelings and maybe even a pet. "Those must be some sad apples you're picking up. You okay?"

And all of a stupid sudden, the words *your doing a really good job* are a glop of blue ink, my tears hitting the secret note like darts. I've got terrible aim but it's bull's-eye today.

"I'm good," I say, smearing my nose across a jacket sleeve. "I'm having an allergic reaction to the mask stuff. I just need a tissue."

Or maybe just my old friend.

A Delirious Pinball That's Made Out of Sugar

(Four and a half weeks till first preview)

I spend most of the cab ride back to rehearsal playing with balled-up mask parts, which is a lot like old rubber cement. The only thing that gets me through school back home is rolling up rubber cement balls between my fingers, which is as much fun as you can have in a school that doesn't have a drama program.

"I'm sorry I'm getting Nathan back so late," the guardian whose name I refuse to learn says to a stage manager by the sign-in board—the only person here in a hallway that's a ghost town. "Traffic was crazy."

"Don't worry about it," the SM says. "Nate, do you have anything in the rehearsal room? Garret and Monica are working over lunch, and they want the room completely cleared."

"Actually," I say, "I think I left my scarf in there"— and without thinking about it, I stroll right into the war zone.

"Ex*cuse* us," I hear, stopping dead. "*What* are you doing in here?"

"My. Scarf." (No, but seriously.)

Monica laughs. "Sorry. We picked it up and started using it as a prop."

"That's so cool!" I say. "Just keep it." I whir on myself and reach for the handle, but my hands are suddenly sweatier than a pop quiz pencil.

"Stay here," Garret says. "We need a body."

A stage manager is pushing a box across the room: "Mr. Charles, I'm sorry. Nate needs to be on lunch. Equity rules."

"Oh, I don't mind, Kiana," I say. Who even knew her name was Kiana? Apparently, I'm able to pull names out of thin air when I'm fighting for stardom. "I already had lunch during my, um, mask fitting." My stomach, on cue, growls. "See. I'm digesting." In reality my stomach is screaming for nourishment, but Garret Charles needs a body. A body's the only thing I've got. Too much of one.

"Come 'ere, puppy," Monica says, patting her knee.

"Whaddya need from me?" I say, running over. "More knee crawls?"

Garret chortles. "Let's never see those knee crawls again, son. Let's have those be something special you only do on wide expanses of prairie."

"So this, *here*," Monica says, cutting in and waving my grey fleece scarf, "is standing in as a girl's coat."

"In the Act One classroom sequence," Garret says, spearing at a salad, chewing on a carrot like he's mad at the thing for being orange, "there's a tricky piece of business between Elliott and the girl."

"The girl he kisses?" I say. There's nothing like that part in the movie *E.T.* Man, there's no improving on that. Come to think of it, why are we trying to improve on that?

"That's right," Garret says. "But we want it to be organic. A bit more danced."

"Fabulous," I *actually* say.

"So," Monica says, facing me, "I'm going to wrap this scarf around your shoulders. You're going to play the girl."

"Hey, don't get any ideas," I say as a joke. But actually, Libby makes me play the girl 80 percent of the time. And 100 percent of the time I don't mind and frankly sort of look forward to it.

"I'll grab one end of the scarf," Monica says, "like it's your sleeve. And I'd love you to chaîné out of it, to your left."

"Sounds great." And a little dangerous. Also: what's a *chaîné*? "A chaîné is like a spinny thing, right?"

"Yes," Garret says, "it's *like* a spinny thing. Hold in *that* stomach"—oh God, he's got a *cane*, and it's poking into my belly—"and spot the corner."

Everyone talks about "spotting" in dance. The only spots I ever see are *after* I've turned.

"Guys," Kiana the stage manager calls over, "you've got five minutes till the actors are back from lunch."

My stomach hears her and gurgles, so to cover up I stammer: "Lemme give the spinny thing a shot," and whip away from Monica so hard, it pulls her over. Scarf and all.

"Wow," she says, breath inches away from my face. She's a smoker and a gum chewer, and that's my favorite smell combo: tar on mint. I know that's not very classy, but it makes me miss my Grandma Flora. "Second time in as many days you've had a girl fall over onto you."

"Reminds me of me when I was his age," Garret says, sticking the cane into the crook of my hand and helping me up. "How about *this*," he says, consulting a pocket watch, which I didn't even know were *made* after World War Zero. "Since we've only got *four* minutes until the actors are back, why don't the two of you switch roles. Nate: Take Elliott. Monica: Take Girl with Coat, or whatever we're calling her."

"Awesome!" I go.

"So," Garret says, "mayhem, mayhem, mayhem . . ." He kind of swirls his hands in the air, representing a bunch of actors. "The teacher faints onto the desk, the wind machine is blowing—"

"Oooh!" I say, "a wind machine! Amazing." I throw my scarf to Monica.

"So we'll count to three, and then you'll grab the

fabric," Monica starts to say—but I'm jogging away from her. "Where are you *going*?"

"Grabbing a box! To play Elliott's desk!" I push over one of the dozen wooden cubes we've got, jumping to the top and catching sight of a wall clock. "We're running out of time!"

Monica laughs and sticks out her arm, and Garret yells, "One," and Monica shouts, "I'm already prepped for 'Three,'" and I hold the scarf tight as she whirls away from me, beautifully. And then: nothing. We stare at Garret for a reaction.

"Interesting," he says, in the same way my science teacher says "Fascinating" when I've decorated my homework margins with flowers. "Monica, if you'd calm the turn down when you're teaching this to whichever child is playing Girl with Coat—"

"Girl with *Jacket*," Kiana hollers, "and it's Hollie. And she and the other actors are waiting by the door, Garret."

"We'll play with all that as the template," Garret says, standing, dumping most of the salad in the trash. "Let's just make sure to have Jordan stand on that box. Not a bad idea, Nate."

"Cool."

Not a bad idea, Nate.

Those words ricochet through my head, bouncing around like a delirious pinball that's made out of sugar. Like a gumball then, I guess.

"Yo, Nate!" Keith runs over from the door. "Where were you on lunch? We missed ya."

"Just in the studio creating another signature moment," I almost go. "Uh—just hanging back," I go instead.

And as the rest of the actors flood in, spilling around us and dropping bags and jackets in the corner, my pinball gumball sugar head is so delirious with Garret's single compliment in this new wind-machine reality, that I barely overhear two of the adult dancers whisper to each other.

"Did you see the piece in the *Post*?"

"No. Who buys newspapers anymore? What's up?"

"Our first controversy at *E.T.: The Musical*."

Stage management claps and whistles, herding the pack. They're all buzzing from lunch.

"*Allegedly* Garret is furious with Dewey."

"Oh?" the other dancer says, pulling on a sweatshirt and beginning a series of warm-up lunges that would send me straight to intensive care.

"*Allegedly*. They disagreed about casting from day one and now the *Post* is reporting that they're thinking of firing an actor . . . somebody they've disagreed with from day one. Plus, we're massively over-budget."

"What was the headline?"

"*Dewey or Die.*"

But she never makes it through the word *Die*,

because just as the *D* is leaving her lips, Dewey strides in—his face as red as E.T.'s glowing stomach.

"Garret," he calls out. "Can I see you in the hallway for a second?"

Garret gathers his jumpsuit, which sits like Peter Pan's shadow, rumpled up in a chair. "By all means," he says. "Monica: Care to carry on with the finale?"

"I'd love to," she says. But she looks nervous.

And as Garret leaves the room, I hear one last thing from the dancer behind me: "Basically, we could be heading into the most expensive flop in history. If somebody doesn't get us some good press, we're all going to be out of a job a week after opening."

We're deep into rehearsals and I finally got my first compliment. *Not a bad idea, Nate.* But maybe it doesn't even matter.

I look around, desperate to see if any of the other kids overheard this critical gossip. But they're busy not listening. They're texting, joking, being regular kids. I wonder what it's like.

"Okay, dancers—and others—let's start with the third section in the finale: wing time steps."

Normally I'd lead the groans. But all I can think about now is my Broadway adventures crashing down in a sad black pile. Just like Peter Pan's shadow.

Paper Towels As Distraction Technique

(Three weeks till first preview)

I'm starting to learn that "the thing" about New York is you can't even go and take an innocent pee without running into trouble.

"Hello, Mommy."

Oh God. Somebody else is in here. Was I saying any of my lines out loud? (Yes, I'm still studying the E.T. lines in a bathroom stall—even if it's almost been a whole week since rumors started swirling that the show might not even run.)

"Everything's good, Mommy. I think the director is very happy."

This kid's mom is screaming through the phone so loudly, I'm self-conscious a woman's in the bathroom with us.

"Yes, Mommy. The publicist said it's looking very likely I'll appear in a *Teen Vogue* spread."

Oh God. *Jordan.*

"And that we'll need an all-new wardrobe for the interview. And speaking of: Which credit card should I use?"

My family barely has one credit card. Jordan's has multiple. One for new cars, one for new outfits, one for miscellaneous purchases over a million dollars.

"Okay, Mommy."

The words are nice but the tone is a little harsh. This kid's Mommy is grilling him, that's for sure. I shift in the stall as quietly as possible.

"Yes, of *course* the other leads loved the cupcakes from Amy's Bread. Just like you said they would."

I roll my eyes so hard, I bet Jordan can hear socket veins straining against themselves.

"I have to go, Mommy. We're staging the last scene and I need to work up something sad in my sense memory."

It's quiet for about twelve seconds, and I hike my feet up just as I hear him crouching to look beneath the stall: almost caught.

"You can do this, Jordan," I hear him say, whispering into the mirror. Then he breathes so heavy it sounds like he's hyperventilating, and I look through the slit in the bathroom door and watch him slap his face *so* hard, it almost makes me miss my bullies back home. One had to admire their incredible aim, if nothing else.

"*Oof. Oof.*" He grunts with each slap, then shakes

it out and stares his beet-red reflection down. "You. Are. Elliott." *Slap*. "Be. Elliott."

I nearly jump off the toilet seat and break up his own fight—Libby and I have a rule about rescuing anyone being bullied, thinking it our sort of secret superhero job to right the world's wrongs. But there's nothing in our rule book about somebody bullying *himself*. And besides, Jordan's moved on to scooping a glop of Vaseline across his bullet-like fangs, flashing a trillion-dollar smile at himself: "*Show* time!"

He shuffles across the locker room to the exit, and when the door shuts behind him in a wheeze, I let the last exchange sink in. This kid beats himself up to prepare for a role. There is so much about the world I still don't understand.

"*Glurp bleep balingo.*"

I start quiet, reviewing all of E.T.'s lines on page six, knowing I'm not needed for another fifteen minutes downstairs. They've basically cut my chorus part back so much, I could practically be a stage manager and at *least* not have to worry about my hair.

"*Glurp,*" I say, staring at the page and then looking away to make sure I have every vowel in the right order. "*Glurp.*" But who am I kidding? I have a photographic memory, all but wasted in the background. And as I'm about to move on to "*bleep,*" I don't even make it to the *b* before—

"Who is that?"

Oh, *Dude*. (The flop. Not the word. I can't say the word *dude* with a straight face. Though, according to my brother Anthony, I can't say anything with a straight anything.)

"Um."

"Come out of that stall. Who's there?"

"Uh."

"Were you *eavesdropping* on me?" There's more worry than fury in Jordan's voice, like the time Dad threatened to barge in on me and Libby after we'd noisily switched outfits in my bedroom. "Come *out*." Jordan's pounding on the stall, harder than you'd think a skinny kid could hit.

"Don't you need to save those fists for your own face?" I almost yell, but don't. I just swipe my feet to the floor and grab my bookbag and script, kicking the door open.

"How long have you *been* in here?" I blurt. (Reverse psychology, a total Libby technique.) "I had my earphones in and . . . and didn't hear a thing."

Jordan scoffs. "Please, Nate. Do you . . . do you even, like, *have* earphones?"

He's right. I don't even have an iPod. Rich kids notice everything.

"Well, sorry for having to pee," I say, shifting my weight and launching to the sink to pump out a few handfuls of paper towels. (Terrible for the environment, but you can stall for *hours* with a few handfuls of paper towels, dabbing at mysterious cracks on your face.)

"You followed me in here, didn't you?" he says.

"I was in here first. I mean, not to be technical, but . . ."

He wiggles his nose so hard, a wedge of hair-sprayed cowlick comes loose, popping straight up and practically making a cartoon *boing*-sound.

"Well, irregardless," he says. "If you overheard me on the phone with my manager, you should have spoken up. Or coughed. Or *something*." His face is practically purple, the slap marks bleeding through like when you practice your autograph in a foggy mirror.

"Wait, your mom is your manager?" I say.

"Oh. Oh, right. I guess I'm getting phone calls mixed up. Pardon me for, like, being a little thrown off. My mom *warned* me about spies, but I didn't believe her."

I can tell he's not used to being mean. You can always tell, because a real bully has a little bit of fear in his eyes, like everything they're saying might be true about themselves. Jordan's eyes are fogged over in the trance of stardom.

"Listen, Jordan: At least your parents let you use their credit cards," I try. "I bet my dad wouldn't let me borrow his if it was the last day on earth."

"Oh, *puh-lease*. My mom told me what part of town you're from. *Jank*burg?" Jordan laughs, the bathroom tiles picking up on the act and ganging up on me, too. *"You can't ask for your parents' credit cards when they haven't even got one."*

But then he winces, like he's expecting *me* to hit *him*. Like he doesn't totally . . . mean what he's saying? My hand muscles make the very opposite of a fist. I drop the paper towels, speechless.

"Boys."

We're caught. I flip my head around so fast, my neck cracks in places I didn't even know existed. The head stage manager towers over us. *"Jordan*, you are three minutes late for rehearsal. And, Nate, why didn't the guardians know where you were?"

"Oh God," Jordan says. "I am so sorry, Roscoe." Jordan's freaked out, turning so many colors, I half-expect to see a pot of gold at his feet. "Are you going to tell Dewey on me?"

"Just get downstairs, Jordan."

Jordan shakes his head at me. "Good luck practicing your E.T. lines in the *bathroom*. Which is, like, the biggest audience you'll probably ever get."

But his voice fades by the end, like he's reaching for words he hasn't quite memorized.

Jordan pushes past Roscoe and tries to slam the door, but it's one of those air-pressurized dealies that closes superslow. All we're left with is a steady back-draft of Jordan's cologne (Drakkar Noir).

"What was that all about?" Roscoe asks.

"I don't know. Maybe Jordan's having a rough day?"

"I'll say," Roscoe says, scratching his chin. "You okay?"

"Oh, me?" I giggle. "*Totally* fine. When somebody talks like that to me back home, I usually end up with a mouth full of toilet water. So this was a piece of cake." God, I'd love a piece of cake right now.

Roscoe gives me the pity face. "You oughtta not hang out in here, Nate-o. We share this bathroom with all the other shows rehearsing in the building. And you need to be with a guardian." It's obvious this guy doesn't work with kids, much. A thirteen-year-old can only get into so much trouble by himself in a bathroom. It's the soccer field where we really need protection. All that *kicking*. "Get downstairs, Nate."

"Sure thing, Roscoe," I say, throwing my bookbag over a shoulder.

"Hey, and Nate? No matter what that kid says, learn those E.T. lines, yeah?"

"Oh, I will. Sure I will." Like I couldn't already recite the entire thing backward already.

"I've done a bunch of shows," Roscoe says.

"Uh-huh?" Of course, now I *have* to pee.

"And you never know when you might have to go on. Please, I've had to stand in for *actors*. In opening *numbers*, on opening *nights*." Roscoe's now leaning into the door, staring off into the wide open space of his career. "Never open a show during a snowstorm, I always say."

"So do I!" I shout for some reason, finally throwing those paper towels away and pushing past Roscoe to the stairwell.

"Oh, and Nate? Check the callboard. Somebody pinned up a note for you."

Adventures on a
Stove Top

(Three weeks till first preview)

Onions are the perfect thing to chop when you're feeling sort of generally sad. When you already want to cry.

"Well, that sounds all right, then. Like a stage manager is on your side."

"Yeah, I guess, Aunt Heidi."

I'm *chop-chop-chopping* away, making the onion portion of my Grandma Flora's famous chili recipe. The last ingredient you add in is a whole bottle of beer, but the alcohol boils off in the heat, so it's not like it's any big deal. Still, Aunt Heidi might let me pour it in, which is cool.

"We could practice lines sometime, if you like?" she says, holding a can of beans like it's made out of rusty nails. (She's not much of a cook.) "You could show me some of the *E.T.* choreography?"

"Oh, thanks," I say, tipping the cutting board into

a pot. Man, I'm actually really good at chopping stuff. I was the star pupil in Home Ec. "But I want to have all my lines down before I show you anything."

"Nate, you're a *star* memorizer. I heard you and Libby quoting entire passages from *Passing Strange* the other day over Skype."

We were actually swearing our heads off—*Passing Strange* was a megaflop, with a surprisingly catchy score—but Heidi's right.

"Thanks," I say, "but it doesn't seem like there's much of a purpose, you know? To going over my lines? I'll never go on for E.T. anyway. Mackey is a minor movie star, and—"

"*Minor,*" Heidi says. "Way minor."

She knows her way around minor actors. Heidi's booked two commercials in the last several months, and I was even around when she got the first one. She calls me her lucky charm, but it's funny because you usually hold lucky charms close, and Aunt Heidi sometimes has a hard time being affectionate.

"And *anyway*," I say, stirring the chili pot, "Asella is such a pro. And they love her. And apparently they only put the first understudies on anyway. So. Yeah."

"What's this all about, Nate? Why are you so worked up? You're still making your Broadway debut!"

God, I wish Freckles were here. Aunt Heidi's roommate. Another guy—and one who really "got" me, because he's an actor, too, and wasn't born in New York. I bonded with him during the great Audition Escape from Jankburg, and here he had to go and get a show out of town. That being said, I get to have Freckles's room, and it has lots of cool drawers to explore.

"I know I'm superlucky," I say. "I feel bad because it's almost like I'm complaining."

"Yes," Aunt Heidi says, "it *is* almost like that."

The phone rings just as I'm debating laying my head inside the oven. Aunt Heidi screens the call and I take a sip of chili.

"Heidi . . . what do you do when something you thought you really wanted turns out to be . . . disappointing?"

"Good Lord, Nate," she says, taking the spoon. "I'm not *that* bad a chef."

Her phone rings a second time, and Heidi goes, "Unknown number again," but picks up. And then: "You bet," she says, "he's right here."

I perk up. My nose stings from all the cayenne pepper steam, but it seems a fitting punishment for such an ungrateful guy.

"Okay. Okay." Heidi twists her ponytail and then disappears into the bedroom with the phone.

Of course. This is it. "They're firing me," I say to the chili pot. In a way, I'm prepared for this and okay with it.

"Hey." She's back. "What's *wrong*, Nate?"

Apparently I'm not prepared for this, and I'm not okay with it.

"Who was that?"

"*E.T.*"

"Uh-huh?" My legs go numb.

"They want you in at nine twenty tomorrow."

I sigh. "For the regular aerobics session?"

"No," Aunt Heidi says, taking a beer from the fridge. "They want you to report straight to the stage managers' office. Something about a meeting with you and that *Jordan*."

"Am I in trouble?" I say, or yell. Good golly: I break Genna in half. I break Jordan's confidence. It's like I'm the wrong kind of secret weapon—one that could go off at any moment.

"Unclear," Heidi says, not pouring the beer into the chili pot at all but instead throwing it back in a sorority-girl gulp. "But we'll make certain you're there at nine twenty sharp. I'm sure it'll be no biggie." But she says the last part so unconvincingly, it's hard to believe she's booked any commercials at all. "Where are you going?" she calls out. "Dinner's almost ready."

"Quick call to make!"

I'm heading to Heidi's room to find Libby on Skype, praying her screen name (SuttonFaster) will flash across the monitor. Instead, I get the resident cat, thumping its tail on Heidi's desk.

"Scram," I say. (But not to get rid of her. Her name is Scram.) "Get lost."

"Five minutes, Nate!" Heidi yells, but I'll need more than that; Libby's not online, so there's only one thing to do—call her on my horrible old phone that barely gets any reception in Heidi's place.

"Hi, Nate." She picks up in one ring.

"Hey, Lib—need your help." She's got amazing strategies for crying on cue, which I could use tomorrow morning when I get taken to task for spying on Jordan in the bathroom. "You got a second?"

But either she's picked up a new instrument or she's blowing her nose, because all I get is a seven-decibel honk.

"Everything okay?"

"God, Greaty, it's really not." I keep waiting for the zinger—the joke—but it doesn't come. "They're taking my mom in for more tests, Natey. She's up and down and it just . . . it doesn't look good."

Here I am, calling my best friend to complain about Broadway troubles, and she's got real ones.

"Libby, I am *so* sorry. What . . . what are you going to do?"

The floorboard squeaks and I turn to see Heidi in the door frame. And maybe it's the way my face looks—probably like a grown-up's, because that's the size of the problem—but she leaves me alone, taking Scram with her and shutting the door.

"I'm not sure," Libby says. "But I have to go in a sec because I'm making Mom dinner."

"Oh, that's nice," I say. Though I've had Libby's version of dinner. It usually involves a toaster.

"Listen, Natey. Enough about my tragedy; gimme some comedy. How's New York Dreamy City?"

I touch my face (don't ask me why) and remember last week—how it felt to be covered in a goopy mask that reminded me of Oatmeal Complexion Healers. Which reminded me, like everything does, of Libby.

"New York Dreamy City . . ." I say, pressing into the divot of my chin, which might be my only genuinely handsome feature. Jordan's got a divot, too, in addition to two unbelievably deep dimples and perfect earlobes that aren't even attached to his head.

"Well, New York is nothing without you, Lib. But it's a pretty good nothing."

"That's amazing."

Oh, just say it Nate. "But, listen: I don't think I've made a single real friend. And not only do I wish I were *playing* the lead, the lead *hates* me. And I'm still too chubby. And I can't tap. And a lot of other 'ands.'"

"You cut out, there, champ," Libby says, huffing a little and probably bounding down the steps to pop a strudel in for Mrs. Jones. "What was that last part?"

The buzzer goes off in Heidi's kitchen. Time to add the beer. Time to get over myself.

"Nothing, Libby. I just said I've . . . made a bunch

of friends. And . . . they're great, but they're no you."

We hang up, and Heidi lets me pour what's left of the beer, and she doesn't even ask me if everything's okay. When you know it's not, and you're an adult, I think you don't even ask. We just sit in silence and somehow make our way through half a pot of chili, in tribute to my long-gone Grandma Flora, back home.

And that gets me thinking. *Home*.

And rather than practice E.T.'s lines—I *know* the lines, for God's sake—I make one more phone call, to the last person who expects to hear from me.

The Last Person Who Expects to Hear from Me

(Three weeks till first preview)

"I'm sorry to call you so late at work."

I'm settled on the edge of a fire-escape step, four floors below Heidi's apartment, dangling my feet into the chilly black.

"Nathan? Is everything okay?"

"Oh, everything's swell, Ma. No problems at all." A rat scurries below, and even though it's probably twenty good yards away, I scream a little.

"What was *that*?" Mom asks.

"Oh, nothing, Mom. Just . . . warming up my voice for rehearsal tomorrow."

"Nate, it's almost nine o'clock at night. Did you already have dinner? Is your aunt keeping you fed? Why are you calling?"

Gee, nothing like a "We really miss you around home" to make a kid feel really missed around home.

"We already had dinner, Ma. Grandma's chili recipe, in fact."

"With the *beer*?" Mom shrieks—as if *she's* not the one who can't be trusted around alcohol.

"Yes. With the beer. But Aunt Heidi poured it herself." (Lies.) "There's no problem here, Ma."

"Then why are you calling? Are you in trouble with the other kids?"

"No, Mom."

I fondle the new folded-up note that my secret admirer gave me. My secret Genna. She drew a cute little cartoon penguin for some reason (probably because that's how I'd look in a tux, which I hope I get to wear for opening night) and had it tacked to the callboard the other day.

"No, I've made a ton of new friends, Mom."

Might not be totally true, but nobody's pushed me into a locker in weeks—not since I left Jankburg—so in a way I've made friends with somebody called Luck.

"Well, that's good, Nathan. It's good to make friends."

Ha. *This has been Sherrie Foster, on friendship.* A lady whose only friends are her flowers, her precious orchids in the garage that if I *so much as look at* will get me a boot so far up my butt, I'll be coughing shoelaces till kingdom come.

"Yup. Everything's hunky-dory here in New York." A car alarm goes off and I wince, covering the mouthpiece. Mom'll freak if she knows I'm on a fire escape, hiding from Aunt Heidi—who never lets me do anything on my own in the city.

"Well, then, why are you calling me on my work line? You know this is my alone time."

It's true. I called Flora's Floras because that's where Mom always hangs out, pruning inventory and counting registers and avoiding Dad.

"I just—I have a favor to ask. I really want to send flowers to Libby."

I pick a chip of paint from the black banister and realize it's not black at all, but a sort of dove white that's covered in industrial revolution soot. This town is so incredible; it's like it takes place in the past and the future all at once.

"Flowers? What for?"

I flick the soot into the courtyard, watching it disintegrate into a hundred parts.

"Because of Libby's *mom*, Mom. She's not doing so hot. I think it would mean a lot to Libby."

Mom sighs the sigh she always sighs when I ask her for something she knows any other (nice) mom would give in to.

"Well, I guess it would be all right," she says. I hear crinkling from the other end and am just sure she's finishing a Chipotle burrito. This was the one thing we bonded over back home: our love of guacamole.

Which is a pretty sophisticated thing for a kid to like, because of the texture and color.

Mom's voice changes: "We could send your friend a Pretty 'n' Pink birthday bouquet for forty-seven dollars, or . . . *hmm* . . . a teddy bear that has a cast on its arm, for twenty-five? Girls go nuts for that."

God. "Mom, I'm trying to *comfort* Libby, not remind her that her mother is dealing with, like, a lot worse than a broken arm."

"Just trying to help," she says, picking at the foil and probably avoiding the red peppers.

"And you're *charging* me, by the way? You're going to *bill* me for these flowers?"

"*Um . . . your father just walked in,*" she whispers. Then, in full voice: "Flowers are a fragile commodity that require upkeep"—she's reading from the disclaimer we've got taped to the store cash register, recited before every sale—"and Flora's Floras is not responsible for decay or damage, Nate."

Just as I'm about to put up a fight—I helped her come *up* with that disclaimer—I hear Dad's voice in the background. "*Is that our boy, Sherrie?*" Oh, no. "*You're not doing an arrangement for free, now, are you?*"

I hear Mom stuttering, and then the phone gets scratchy and—

"Nathan? This is your father."

"Hello, my father," I nearly say.

"You know the policy here. Blood is thicker than water but Miracle-Gro is thicker than blood."

"Yep."

"And more expensive."

"Yeah, Dad, I know."

"We can't go giving out free arrangements. Not with how business is doing."

Business is *not* doing, is what he means by that. These days people just take screen shots of floral bouquets and send them to their friends virtually. No decay or damage there.

"And with the kind of money you're pulling in, son, you might do well to send *us* a little money on the weekends."

He's not kidding, but I almost laugh. The only thing I even do on the weekends is watch a few YouTubes on Heidi's computer and then go to *work* myself.

"Libby's mom is *dying*, Dad," I say, rising to my feet on the fire escape. I never sit when I'm on the phone with Dad, because it's the only time I get to practice what it feels like to stand up to him. "And I was *thinking* it would be nice to send her some flowers. Is all."

I hate when I sound like him. Using somebody's else's bad fortune for my own argument.

"That is indeed a lovely thing, son," he says. Too nicely. This is about to get complicated. "But I'm sorry to say I just can't figure out the math on this one."

"Gee, Dad," I want to say, "I'd have thought you'd be beside yourself with joy that I want to send flowers to a *girl*."

But instead I just go: "I'll send money. As soon as I get my next *E.T.* check, I'll have Heidi send money for whichever arrangement Mom thinks is nicest."

"He's come to his senses, Sherrie," Dad says, handing the phone back and loping away.

Our TV must be on the fritz at home. There's nothing like the sight of my dad watching a big game at Mom's shop, with his head surrounded by a bunch of petunias. It's a riot.

"I'll say good-bye, then," I hear Mom go to Dad as she takes the receiver back. I bet he didn't even make eye contact with her. *"Thanks."*

I forget where I am for a second, the suffocating nylon blanket of my parents' voices dulling my senses. That's why I'm so surprised to feel a hand on my shoulder.

"Okay then, Natey," Mom says—for a second I think it's actually *her* behind me—"I'll send Libby the bear. Without the arm cast."

But I barely hear any of the last part, because Heidi is dragging me back up the fire escape.

"*Who* are you on the *phone* with?" she says, pushing Freckles's window open.

"Your sister," I whisper.

Heidi's eyes go wider than the winter moon, and she mouths, "Don't say anything." I know what she means. Mom would kill Heidi if she knew I were scaling buildings in Manhattan. Even if, technically, this is Queens.

"It should be there Tuesday," Mom says. "Okay?"

Apparently I forget to respond—perhaps distracted by how deeply my aunt's nails are digging into my aunt's nephew's forearm.

"*Nate?*"

"Night, Mom," I manage to utter without squealing.

"Night, Nathan. Hey, Nathan?"

"Hey, Mom?"

"I . . . *we miss you.*" Her voice gets quiet, or maybe just tired. "And I love you lots. We could use your good energy around the shop."

"I . . . love you lots too, Ma. Mom."

I hang up the call and feel my Nokia burning extra warm in my hand. Maybe the battery is just overused. Or maybe it's just smoking-hot because Mom said something nice to me.

They miss me.

"To *bed*, mister. And *never* go out there again."

But Heidi doesn't have to worry about that. My shins are scuffed, my hands are covered in soot, my face is an oily sweat slick.

"New York One says it's thirty degrees out tonight," Heidi yells from the bathroom. "You're lucky Scram wandered into the bedroom after you, and I found her. If you'd gotten stuck out there overnight, you would have frozen."

Before Libby's mom got sick, they had enough money to send Libby to a dermatologist. She said they'd freeze her really bad zits off. Maybe if I had gotten stuck on the fire escape overnight, my face would have turned into a perfect, unmarked icicle. If I'd died, at least I'd have died with good skin.

I would have died like Jordan.

Awake at Dawn—and *Not* to Watch Cartoons

(Two weeks and six days till first preview)

It's a tough thing to fall asleep when the threat of a big morning meeting looms over you like a Geography quiz. When my alarm goes off, I've barely gotten any rest at all, after boiling the night away in Freckles's striped flannel sheets. I yawned my way through breakfast, yawned and nodded off on the subway to work, yawned and nodded off and hit rapid eye movement in the elevator, and now—finally—am jolted to life when I see Jordan. He's sitting in a chair in the hallway outside the stage managers' office, stone still, like he's waiting for a dentist appointment.

(During which—I guarantee you—they wouldn't find a single cavity.)

"Hi."

"Hey," he barely says, at work studying his script. Doesn't he know his lines by now?

"We'll miss you in cardio-aerobics, Nate!"

Monica's passing me, holding a giant bouncy ball. At every morning session she's got a new contraption to whip us into shape. Last week, she laid out yoga mats and had us do something called a Downward Dog. It didn't look like my dog Feather at all, who'd probably chew a yoga mat to shreds or just curl up and snooze. I could use a snooze right now. I could use Feather, too.

"Look alive," says a guardian as stage management's door cracks open.

"Hi, boys," says the head stage manager, Roscoe, with that moustache you could hide from your parents in. "We're finalizing the day's rehearsal schedule and will just be another minute."

"That's fine, Roscoe," Jordan says in a dull drone, eyes not looking up from his lap.

"Jordan, why don't you keep looking at those new pages—I know a lot of new material came in overnight. And Nate . . ."

Roscoe tilts his head, figuring out how to instruct me.

"Sit-ups," Monica says, tossing the bouncy ball into the aerobics room and disappearing after it.

"Perfect," Roscoe says, scratching at his moustache, which sheds entire clumps of hair and stray breakfast. "Do some sit-ups or something, Nate."

I drop to the floor and try to remember how

Anthony approaches sit-ups in the garage. (*He's allowed near Mom's beloved orchids.*)

"New pages?" I say to Jordan. Stalling.

"Yeah," he says. Actually he just kind of mouths it, busy closing his eyes and memorizing the updated script. The *text*. I bet he calls it *the text*.

"Like: *more* new *script* pages?"

"Yes, Nate," he says, flicking over to me. His hands are shuddering a little. "They changed almost the entire second-act scene where I find E.T. in the ravine."

Where *he* finds E.T. in the ravine. Dear Lord. It's like Jordan thinks he *is* Elliott. Am I right? Am I right, here?

"The librettist," Jordan says, "didn't think the scene was funny enough."

"There weren't enough *laughs* in a scene where you find your best friend nearly dead in a ditch?"

Jordan *actually* almost giggles, which takes me by such surprise, I flinch. I probably haven't gotten a laugh since Libby and I were together last, and this excitement jumpstarts my sit-ups.

"I'm just doing what I'm told," Jordan says. He holds up an old script page, highlighted and crossed out and highlighted again with a different color marker, his blocking scribbled and erased and rewritten in the margins. "It's a lot to keep up with. We've got the designer run-through on Friday and they just rewrote *half* the words to my song with E.T. in the third scene."

Those *were* some pretty lame lyrics. Nobody could keep a straight face when Jordan tried to pull off the word *planet* rhyming with *man up*.

"Besides," he says, switching to his old tone, "aren't you keeping up on the script changes? E.T. has a bunch of new . . . well, I wouldn't exactly call them *lines*, since they're basically just grunts. But still. You should check your folder."

All the actors have their own folder, like a personal mailbox in the hallway, where stage management slides in our updated script pages every morning. The creative team is rewriting this show so often, there's barely time to keep up with the *old* material, let alone the new stuff. Still, I only have to watch Mackey "grunt" something once, and I've got it.

"Yeah, I guess I should check out my folder," I say (standing up from my *fifth* sit-up, which was my best one). I'm reaching for the new pages when I catch sight of Monica in the studio, making Asella balance on one foot on top of the blue ball. Yikes, Monica is a slave driver, if slave drivers dyed their hair stop-sign red.

"Boys," Roscoe says, finally opening the door, "let's get going."

Jordan and I bump into each other on the way in (we can't even coordinate offstage entrances, let alone onstage) and find two seats opposite Roscoe in the office.

"So," he says, taking a big gulp of coffee, which spills into his moustache and is immediately absorbed, like some kind of organic ShamWow. "You probably know what this is about."

"I just want to say something," I hear my mouth say. Then I feel my throat gulp and witness my fists tighten. "I'm really sorry. About the other day. In the bathroom."

Roscoe looks concerned—like a principal, practically. Usually when I'm in the principal's office, I'm waiting for an apology from James Madison or one of his henchmen. It's weird to *be* the bully this time.

"To explain: I was in the bathroom making phone calls, and I should have let Jordan know I was overhearing his conversation. I wouldn't say I was *spying*, because I wasn't *planning* on overhearing anything. But still. I should have, like, spoken up just as soon as I heard Jordan having his panicked phone call. With his Mommy."

God, it's so easy to turn into a jerk when you've been accused of being one.

"*Please,*" Jordan says under his breath.

"O . . . *kay*," Roscoe says, checking the time on his

phone, as our castmates begin filtering out of the elevator. "That's . . . nice, Nate. But this isn't about that."

"It isn't?" Jordan and I both say. I'm not sure which one of us is more shocked.

"No," Roscoe says. "This is about a big press event coming up."

Assistant stage manager Kiana knocks on the door and says, "Five minutes" to Roscoe. God, I wish the five-minute warning could be implemented at school back home. You can handle anything for five minutes, even mistaken apologies. Even History class.

"As you know, Jordan," Roscoe says, "we're going to be doing a giant outdoor event—Broadway at Central Park—to be televised live the day before previews start." He pulls up a file on the computer. "It's a big publicity opportunity for the show."

"I'm feeling great about that event," Jordan says. But his voice is shaking. "My mom says that's one of the most important events of the Broadway season." Now it's not just his voice that's shaking. His chair looks like it's actually levitating, like maybe *he's* an alien.

"Yes." Roscoe laughs. "The producers have elected to have you sing your Act One song, Jord. You know that already."

"I do," *Jord* says.

"But now that the lyrics have all been changed around—"

"Yes," Jordan says, "I've stayed very up-to-date on the lyrics."

"Fantastic," Roscoe says in an I-don't-really-care way. (The other day, I overheard him saying he misses the old days, when the only children who appeared in musicals "were in the background or dead by the second scene.")

"It's definitely really, *really* important for everyone to keep up on their new pages," Jordan says. He is leaning so far forward toward me that he looks like Feather pointing his nose at a dead mouse in the bushes.

Here, I am embarrassed to report, I squeak. "I *totally* look at my new pages. Very often. I do." Weak.

"Regardless," Roscoe says, standing and shutting off the computer monitor, "now that the song is more about E.T.'s journey to earth, and thus features, you know, *E.T.* more"—Roscoe is barely stifling a yawn, and clearly takes E.T.'s journey to earth about as seriously as my dad takes my journey to Broadway—"we're not sending you to the event alone, Jordan."

"You're *not*?" Jordan says. Here, he stands, flipping the hulking script, from his lap, onto Roscoe's desk, where it lands in a quiet *whoosh*. Sheesh. Even this kid's accidents are elegant.

"No, we're not," Roscoe says, growing restless. "The producers want E.T. there. They think kids will like it more." He puts air quotes, with his fingers, around the words *kids* and *like*.

"Well fine, then," Jordan says. "Where's the part about Nate?" He juts his thumb out at me, hitchhiker style. Man, would I love to see Jordan try to climb into a truck.

"Mackey only does events where he sings solo," Roscoe says. "It's in his contract."

Jordan begins hopping up and down, *actually* hopping up and down and causing the air to stir a bit. Loose sheets of script scatter to the floor like mutant snow. "I didn't know that was an option," he says. "That's a contract option?"

"Relax, Jordan," Roscoe says.

Kiana peeks her head in. "You can keep Jordan, Rosc, but Nate's due in a vocal rehearsal. An important one."

(I love the idea of any Broadway rehearsal *not* being important. Please. This is the only important thing happening on earth, other than late-night SpongeBob marathons.)

"I'll send Nate along in just a sec," Roscoe says.

"Okay, so no Mackey," Jordan says. "Fine. You'll send Asella, right? She's hilarious."

"Asella turned down the event," Roscoe says, just like that—and then turns to me. "So, Nate, all *you* have to do is stand there. It's a nice pay bump—like a whole extra week's salary."

Ummmmmmmmmmmmmmmmmmmwhat?

"Why did Asella say no?" I watch my mouth say in the mirror. There's a mirror in this office. They've mirrored everything in New York. I'm surprised you can't see your own reflection on toilet seats, but they're probably getting around to it any day now.

"Oh, Asella gave some obscure excuse," Roscoe says—and then rolls his eyes. "But we *all* know Asella . . ." As if Asella even talks to me and not *down* at me. Which is a remarkable skill, considering she's the only living adult who's shorter than Nate the Underdeveloped King of Sweets. "She's at the age where actors refuse to do events that take place outside in the dead of winter."

But *I'm* not. I'm the perfect age for outdoor events. When Libby and I practice songs in my backyard, sometimes we *wait* till the dead of winter, because "comedy is best when it's done in the cold," according to Libby. Apparently the threat of frostbite gives every punch line a little jolt, because if you don't laugh, your body will shut down or something.

"Has anyone even taught Nate the blocking?" Jordan says, sounding desperate.

"You're just going to stand there and sing the song, Jordan," Roscoe says, putting a hand on his shoulder. "We're not even doing the part where you hop from the bed to the dresser, putting the hula skirt on E.T."

"But that's where I get my *laughs*," Jordan says, shrugging Roscoe's hand away.

"Well, to be *fair*, Jordan, I think Mackey's getting most of the laughs there. But you sing the song beautifully, and the Central Park event is on a makeshift riser. There won't be any set pieces. Nate will just stand there."

"Even Alien Number Seven can handle that," I say too loudly, like we're all friends enjoying a bowl of communal popcorn.

"I can't believe this," Jordan says. Stealing the words from my frontal lobe.

I'm going to make a week's salary for just standing still. It's like I finally understand what I've been practicing for in gym class.

"Does he even have, like, a costume that fits him?"

"Jordan, this conversation is over. And you're not being a very gracious star." Roscoe opens the door. "This shoots right after tech rehearsals are over. It goes live and it goes national. A huge audience, probably over eight million people. I'm going to send an e-mail to your parents to confirm time and place."

"Cool." *Over eight million people.* Jankburg has less than eight *thousand*. And that's including the cemeteries.

"My mom's going to flip out that I'm not doing this performance alone," Jordan says. "I mean . . . no offense, Nate." Now he's all-out frowning.

"Break it up, you two," Roscoe says. "Nate, get upstairs to music rehearsal. Jordan, study that new packet. You've got a lot of lines and I'd be more worried about *those* than your co-star."

"He isn't my co-star; Mackey is," Jordan says, but he's whispering it to himself. "Oh, God, if we mess up *anything* on national TV, my mom'll kill me."

"I'll let your mom know Nate is a very responsible kid and everything's going to be just fine," Roscoe says. But I barely hear the last part, because he's literally kicking my butt out the door.

Jordan's mom will kill him if I mess him up on national TV. I'm not even sure my parents will tune *in*.

But as I'm hopping up the stairs to music rehearsal, two at a time, I'm not thinking about that. This isn't about my parents or Jordan's parents or even Jordan, who looked genuinely frightened back there. Like he might get into a kind of trouble James Madison gives me back home if I trip him up.

No, this isn't about any of that.

This is about me making my national television debut—and a whole week's salary on top of it—playing the title role of a Broadway musical.

Move over, Annie.

Make way, Oliver.

Step aside, Jordan.

(Here comes Nate.)

Oohs and Aahs

(Two weeks and six days till first preview)

I bet you'd be surprised by all the wasted space in a Broadway musical's choral practice room. Today we're geared up to learn new parts to the Act One finale, where Elliott and his brother pretend to take E.T. out to go Trick-or-Treating, but really they're heading into the woods. (As if real kids would avoid candy for trees.)

"Okay, actors. Come on in."

The point is that this room is massive, with gleaming wooden floors that lead to mile-high ceilings. This morning it feels like I'm practically up there, floating over the whole room—with the promise of a national television appearance just past the next cloud.

"Whoa, check out Nate." Is that Keith talking? Or just a cloud?

"Naaaate. *Nate*." Hollie's laughing now. Apparently I'm staring at myself in the mirror, and grinning, and sort of . . . swaying.

Keith claps in my face. "Earth to Nate, what-up?"

It's the perfect phrase because that's exactly where I am—on another planet. Not even an astronaut could snap me from this delirium.

"Goofball," Genna says, brushing past us. Okay, that does it.

"Long story, guys," I say to Hollie and Keith—sort of loud enough for Genna to hear—and we all start to giggle. "Some other time." You've just got to be very careful sharing a big secret (*over eight million people*) with a couple of kids. Great as these two might be.

"You guys," says Sammy, the music assistant, flicking through Tweets on his iPhone, "let's quiet down and grab our seats. This is a big rehearsal."

Again with the big rehearsal business.

"I need my sopranos down front and my altos just to the side of them." Everything is "my my my" on Broadway. There's a lot of territory disputes, like a junior high school cafeteria but with more glitter. "And then let's get our baritones in the back with the tenors and basses scattered, or whatever." Sammy always gives up by the end of a simple set of orders.

"Where do you want me?" Keith says. Keith can sing any part, I swear to you. He's got a voice like a Aretha Franklin, who is allegedly his distant aunt, FYI.

"We'll see where we need you," Sammy say. "Just grab a chair with the other boys."

Keith and I take seats next to each other, and I pull out my music binder (which is bigger than your average History textbook—even if these days, I do my schoolwork online) and flip to the end of Act One in the score. I haven't had much to sing in the show so far, so who knows what today has in store? Who cares, even. I'm going to be on national TV, if anyone has forgotten.

"So, here's the deal," Sammy says, putting his iPhone down. This must be serious. Musicians never put their iPhones down. "The lyricist has rewritten the Act One closing number."

"Again?" Asella shouts. She's sitting on her music binder, but not to boost herself up, I don't think. Out of protest.

"Yes," Sammy says. "Again."

"What's wrong with an *ooh* and an *aah*?" Asella says to nobody in particular. "I paid for two apartments throughout all of the eighties with a bunch of *oohs* and *aahs*."

"Fair enough," Sammy says, putting his hands up in a "Don't shoot the messenger" plea. "But I'm following orders here."

"Let's get cracking then," Asella says. "I'm hardly keeping up on all the new changes, as it is." She points to her seat, the binder's pages barely staying inside.

"So, my tenors," Sammy says. "Same as before—

we're still going from the B-flat at measure fifty-two to the C-sharp in fifty-four, and holding it."

"Forever," says one of the tenors—the guy who appeared in the entire original run of *Les Misérables* and is thus the unofficial mayor of Broadway, to me anyway. I've been studying him in rehearsals. "We hold the C-sharp forever."

"We should get hazard pay for that C-sharp," says another tenor.

"Great," Sammy goes, barreling on. "Except— here's the change, everyone—instead of singing *aah* on the C-sharp, we're going to sing, *flyyyyyy*."

"Fly?" the first tenor says, looking around like Sammy just spilled Coke Zero on his favorite sweater. "We're singing the word *fly*?"

"You're singing *fly*," Sammy says, fiddling with a pencil and looking as if he's about to stab himself, already. We're fifteen minutes into a long music rehearsal and there's already a warm debate that's hinting at hot.

"Let's get this straight," Asella says. "Just to clarify, as storytellers. We're sending a bunch of kids into the woods and we're telling them to 'fly'?"

"Look," I hear. We flip our heads around to see Dewey hiding in the corner of the room, chewing on a pen cap. His chin is streaked with blue ink. "Look, everyone. Listen up." He sorts of dares himself to move and then jump-starts so fast that he trips over a sneaker. He never ties his sneakers. My kind of adult. "So, yeah." In two seconds he's next to the piano. "I know. A lot of changes."

"A *ton* of changes," a soprano says—one I've been avoiding in rehearsals, because she only makes eye contact with other adults.

"But the changes are all really important," Dewey says.

"*Fly* is going to get us the Tony?" Asella says.

I really can't believe how brazen these people are. If Dewey told me to set my shirt on fire, I'd probably say, *Do you want that stage left or stage right?*

"I don't know if *fly* is getting us the Tony or what," Dewey goes, running a hand through hair that looks like it hasn't been washed since the *movie* of E.T. "What I know is that we're about to move into the theater. And there's a lot of pressure to get this right before we leave the rehearsal rooms."

A lot of pressure always means a lot of money. Dad's always saying Mom's under a lot of pressure at the store, but what else can that mean but money, when you're surrounded by tulips all day? What kind of pressure does a tulip offer?

"Listen," Dewey says. "The composer and lyricist are staying up all night trying to nail this. Rewriting around the clock."

"May I say something?" a baritone offers.

"Sure," Dewey says, momentarily distracted by his hand getting stuck in a clump of bangs. It looks quite complicated up there.

"Perhaps," the baritone continues, "the problem with all the rewriting is that the writers haven't been given the chance to actually *hear* us *do* their most recent material."

He has a point, this giant baritone. We've rehearsed entire scenes that the writers never even watched us perform before they redid all the lines. And as these days have piled on—while I observe everything with wide eyes and closed lips—sometimes it does feel like we just change stuff willy-nilly. Like how Libby'll put a tank top on in the winter just to get attention from the track team.

"I hear you," Dewey says, finally breaking that hand free. It appears as if he lost his wedding band in there. "But you . . . have to trust me."

Nobody says it.

Nobody says why, but the room is so thick with everyone thinking it that it just about breaks Dewey down. His eyes well up and he looks at Sammy and then accidentally starts talking again. "Guys, we're in the theater next week. Once we're onstage, we won't have time to rework stuff. We have to focus on adjusting the lights and doing the sound and making sure it's all, like, superbright and superboomy." Uh-oh. He's talking video game–speak again. "So learn these new parts so that we can forget them, yeah?"

"Let's start with the sopranos," Sammy says, fast. "At measure fifty-four, on *fly*."

"But, *Dewey*," the baritone says, raising his hand as if he's waiting to be called on, but continuing to talk anyway. Classic schoolroom move. "I think the actors' issue is that we learn something one day, it changes the next, and we're losing confidence that we're going to arrive at anything coherent."

Keith and Hollie look at each other and nod vigorously. I take their cue and nod too. It's just what friends *do*, okay?

"Getting confident is what previews are for," Dewey says, but it comes out like a question. Like maybe Garret Charles coached him to say that, or he read it last night in a book called *How to Direct a Broadway Musical*.

"Well *I* for one think it's all poppycock," says an alto. Altos always have funny words for things, especially this one, a British woman who just got her green card. (According to a conversation I overheard the other day. While pretending to be interested in a new game Keith was showing me on his iPhone.) "I will feel silly singing *fly* when not a single soul is even in the air."

I know what these people are doing. They're bullying Dewey. I can spot it a mile away. Or a foot away, which is usually where a bully's taunts are in proximity to my ears.

"You know what, guys?" I say. One of my vocal cords looks at the other one, like, *What are you doing?* And yet: "I think maybe we should just do it."

Dewey looks at me and swallows.

"I mean. What have we got to lose? Everyone's trying, like, their hardest. And we might as well just learn our new parts because, like. We just should." This is my version of a pep talk. Yet another reason I'll never be a gym teacher. "We *just* should," I say again, changing the emphasis. Doesn't seem to help.

"Good God," some adult whispers.

"*I'll* say," somebody else not-whispers.

"Thank you, Jake," Dewey says.

"It's *Nate*," Keith mutters.

"Right," Dewey says. "Right. Nate."

"If the kid wants to sing *fly* so badly," says Asella, making a giant show of looking at her giant-for-Asella watch, "why don't you just give it to the kid?"

Wait . . . *what?* "Oh, that's okay," I say, holding up my music. "It says here *sopranos*."

"You got this, Nate," Keith says. "Nate can totally twerk this out." Keith's words are as alien as E.T.'s.

"You wanna try it as a solo, Nate?" Sammy says.

"Nate, Nate, Nate," a chubby alto tries. She's never said my name before but is suddenly caught up in the action.

"Foster for Prez!" Hollie blurts.

"Oh, I don't know," I say, because I really don't.

"Well, it can't hurt," Sammy says. "Since nobody else seems willing to sing it."

"*I'd* try it," the British alto says. She understudies the Mom role and is forever looking for standout opportunities. "I'd gladly try it as a solo. I didn't realize it was a solo."

"You're an *alto*, Melba," Sammy says. "Give it a shot, Nate. This is your chance to shine on the cast album."

Um.

"Say that again," I say, or my thoughts do.

"The cast album. The original cast album."

"You didn't know we're recording a cast album?" Keith says. He's chewing gum so toxic green, it burns my eyes when I look at him. But maybe I'm just crying a little. "You always record the cast album right after opening night."

"Always," Genna says. She is looking right at me, and playing with her hair.

"I guess I didn't—I guess I hadn't heard that confirmed."

Libby and I dreamed of it, the chance for my voice

to forever be captured in cast-album glory, available for illegal ten-cent download. But to hear it spoken aloud. . . .

"I'd love to try the solo," I say, standing.

"Whoa, he's standing," a tenor says.

"Great," Sammy goes. "Okay, measure forty-five, you're doing the *oohs*."

"The part that switches to dotted eighth notes?"

I'm no expert at music terms, but I've picked up on the biggies, having recorded every one of these vocal rehearsals on Heidi's old tape recorder. You bet I sleep with her earbuds glued in every night, blasting the day's rehearsals back to me. Sometimes I wake up hearing a high-pitched buzz, and it's not even my alarm.

"Dotted eighth notes," Sammy confirms. "You got it."

"Three minutes till lunch," Kiana the stage manager calls out.

Asella goes, "Let's get on with it, then. And breathe, kid. This isn't *American Idol*." She turns to April, beside her: "Nobody knows how to support their voices anymore."

She isn't wrong. Libby and I lose our voices during every sleepover we belt our way through. But still. I've got this. I can hit *any* note if it's just one time. That's why I always sing the Tarzan call at the end of "Defying Gravity" when Libby and I trade off on Elphaba and Glinda.

"Here we go," Sammy says, plunking the intro.

In this section, Elliott sings, *"Gotta get to the woods before Mom finds out."* And his brother Michael answers—stupidly, it's a stupid lyric—*"Gotta get outta here 'fore E.T. starts to shout."* And the ensemble sings *oohs* and *aahs* underneath. I've practiced it a bajillion times.

And so naturally I come in perfectly on time with my *oohs*. This would be an ideal moment to latch on to my rabbit foot for strength, but Libby needs it more than I do. So I quickly touch the penguin cartoon in my pocket, the drawing from Genna. (A boy on a soprano solo needs all the luck he can get—even if he's relying on the wrong animal.)

The music rumbles louder, louder.

"Keep those *oohs* going!" Sammy shouts.

"Breathe!" Asella screams, standing on her chair and pointing to her stomach, as if she holds a reserve of oxygen I can borrow.

"In bar fifty-four," Sammy says, his mouth frothing, "instead of the *aahs*, sing *flyyyyyyyyyy*."

"Breathe!" the entire tenor section says in unison.

"Go, boy," Keith shouts. *"Get* it."

I go. I get it. I get to fifty-four and do just as I've been told. "Fly" is no problem—it's a wide open vowel, easy to just let your jaw go and scream it out. And heck, this word makes *perfect* sense to me in the context of the scene. Of *course* we're not telling E.T. to literally fly away; we're *foreshadowing*. Maybe this is a *great* lyric, if I get to sing it on a cast album.

And we're approaching that great lyric now.

"Flyyyyyy!" I sing, my voice filling the room like a tidal wave of melted caramel.

Or, no. Not at all.

"Flyyyyyy!" I *go* to sing. But don't. Because something goes haywire. Worse than haywire. Hay-on-fire-wire.

Just as I've come to totally believe in this lyric rewrite—making the *F* with my lips, the *L* with my tongue—my voice trips on itself. Cracking in half. Shattering like every record Anthony ever beat in swim class.

I try to sing *Flyyyyyy*, but it comes out, *fl-hack-hack-hack.*

Sammy stops playing.

Dewey stops smiling.

"Actors, you're on lunch."

(I went to Broadway and all I got was this lousy voice change.)

And my heart stops beating.

Stairwell Races and You Won't Believe Who Wins

(Two weeks and six days till first preview)

The back stairwell beckons. Kids like me always know about hidden stairwells, and I slip into its cement-lined chamber, with eight floors of steps and no windows in sight. Just the jail cell in the sky an idiot like me deserves, sentenced to a life of one low voice and no parts to play.

Who's going to cast *me* as Inspector Javert?

"Oh God," I say, pacing, hiding. Everyone's off to lunch but I'm too nauseated to eat. Instead I'm clutching my phone, calling Libby but not getting a signal. (There's no such thing as reception in prison.)

"You okay?" I hear. This lady from another show at our rehearsal studio is taking the stairs to the lobby. "Are you waiting for your parents?"

"No," I say, instinctively hunching over, which is what animals do in the wild when they don't want people to see them crying. "I just lost my contact.

And I'm looking for it. My contact." Smooth, Nate.

"Okay," the lady goes, heading past and then stopping. "Do you need help looking?"

"Please, no," I say. "Honestly. I just need some space."

"Suit yourself," she says, bounding away. I wish I *could* suit myself. If I could suit myself, all my waistbands would be made of elastic. Then, I wouldn't be so constantly reminded of my pear-shaped body, which hasn't even decided which fruit it's going to turn into. Who *knows* if I'm overweight or not? What does overweight mean if you haven't stopped growing? I'm a *genius* weight—practically stick thin—for a six-foot-tall guy, which I may very well become if my body echoes my changing voice.

"Oh God, my *voice*," I say, sitting on a stair.

"It's not such a bad voice."

I look up. "Oh." Ugh. "Hey."

"Hello there, soprano soloist."

"Aren't you on lunch, Asella?"

"Aren't *you* a little spitfire, Nate? Or is it *Jake*?"

She sits next to me, putting a bag down and pulling out a banana. Grown-ups are forever eating fruit.

"Ha. It's Nate. But maybe I should just change it to Jake. Or not even have a name. Maybe I should just go by Anonymous Foster."

"Anonymous Foster sounds like a speakeasy,"

Asella says, peeling back the banana and taking a big chomp. "You turned all sorts of colors when your voice cracked, back there."

She hasn't spoken two words to me the whole rehearsal period. It's like now that I'm officially a loser, I'm safe territory. Anybody could feel good around me.

"That wasn't a voice crack, Asella. That was a voice fail. That was a voice . . . *kaboom.*"

"I coach people on voice, you know."

"I didn't know. I'm not surprised. I overheard you singing all the E.T. songs." (You and you alone, I might add.)

"Yes, well." She yacks up a piece of banana. "It's paying the bills. And it better. I got a lotta bills."

A group of dancers from another show moves between us, but we keep talking.

"You know what you could use?" Asella says.

"A good baritone solo?" I say, picking off the end of my shoelace.

"Exercise," she says, throwing the banana into her bag. "Come on, let's take the stairs to the lobby. I'll race you."

Great, another adult hounding me about cardio. Plus: racing a little person is like asking a toddler to do a counting contest to a hundred. There's no way I won't beat . . . oh, *wait,* Asella's already ten feet ahead of me.

"Come *on*, kid," she says, "let's burn off some of that embarrassment."

"Why are you talking to me?" I shout. "This is freaking me out." Except picture all that with more gasping and the nagging *whap* of my bookbag slamming my lower back every third step.

"Because I need some help," Asella says, spinning like a dust cloud ahead of me. "And I think you might be the guy."

I bang my elbow into a stair rail, groan *Bobbi Boland* under my breath (closed in previews; starred an old-timey blonde called Farrah Fawcett), and genuinely try to catch up with Asella. Man, this lady is like a can of Jolt wearing spectacles and Keds. "Why do you need my help?"

"Look," she says, putting on the brakes without warning (reminds me of Mom in the Caravan). I nearly trip over Asella on the landing between floors two and three, proud of myself for almost beating her. She's breathing hard and practically panting. "I've got bad news and good news and then more bad news and then potential good news." Her cheeks puff like pillowcases on a drying line.

"O . . . *kay*."

"Which should I start with?"

"I don't know. I got confused."

Asella leans against the wall and removes a shoe,

jabbing her knuckles into a bunion that looks remarkably like Lyndon B. Johnson (I did a report on him). "Okay, bad news first."

I crouch and take a deep breath.

"Listen," she says. "Jordan's mom is refusing to let him do this ridiculous outdoor promo unless *I'm* there playing E.T."

She pauses to let that sink in. It sinks in.

"What?"

"His mom thinks I'll make him look good. She's nervous. It's just because I'm old."

I feel the blood rush from my face and swirl around my empty belly, which babbles in protest. "What are you *talking* about?"

"But *listen*, kid. There's someplace I've really gotta be that morning."

I thought she had bills to pay. "What could be so important that you'd skip a whole extra paycheck?"

"Oh, kid, it's boring stuff. Grown-up stuff. Small-claims-court, my-ex-husband-wants-custody-of-my-beloved-dog, not-over-my-small-dead-body stuff."

Whoa. "Oh."

"Besides. They just want me to *stand* there while Jordan sings, which I find kind of insulting. E.T. is the title role. It ain't called *Elliott: The Musical.*"

Hear, hear! But still: "And Mackey isn't doing the event because of, what, something about his contract?"

"Well, who knows with Mackey," Asella says, rolling her eyes and pulling out an apple. The lady has an entire produce section in there. "He's a loose cannon. Hasn't been onstage in *years*. He's a little *unpredictable*, Nate, and that's what the media is reporting, if you're keeping tabs." She waits for me to answer, and appears to realize I'm not keeping tabs: "Garret and Dewey were *very* split-down-the-middle on hiring Mackey."

My God. Maybe Garret wanted to hire . . . *me*.

"Garret wanted to hire *me*," Asella says, side-eyeing me.

"But Dewey won out," I say, "and Mackey got the role instead."

"Mackey doesn't do events. But they're hoping he'll pull in the video game audience, once we open." She laughs.

Turns out Mackey starred in a bunch of Dewey's games, donning a motion-capture suit to play an owl and a dancing bush and a warlock, and everything. He was recently named Motion-Capture Actor of the Decade, according to Keith. Mackey is somewhat of a celebrity among normal boys my age.

"Your forehead is sweaty," Asella says. "It was only four flights of stairs," she has the nerve to add.

"It's not the stairs. It's that . . . flipping *Jordan*, who has the *gall* to take this opportunity away from me."

"Yes. Boys will be boys—even if his mother is

leading the charge. Here's the thing: I—I just can't be there. And I assume you're *dying* to do the event."

Close. I'm *living* for it. For it and it alone. "I guess."

"So how about we make a trade," she says. She takes a bite of the apple, frowns at it like it's a fruit, and leads me downstairs after folding it into a napkin. "We'll stick you in the E.T. costume, say it's me, and you'll get all the glory. After we split the cash."

I chuckle, here. "You're crazy! I'll get in total trouble. I'll get, like, Broadway-grounded."

"No you won't. I've known Roscoe for years." She *does* seem chummy with stage management. "He couldn't care less about rules." She stops just after we exit into the lobby, launching into a conspiratorial whisper: "We toured together in the second national of *Show Boat*, and let me tell you: I've got photos of Roscoe at a bar in Reno that'll have him doing favors for me until *Wicked* closes."

"*Wicked*'s closing?" I say, or scream.

"Relax. It's an expression."

Hollie and Keith are just leaving the building, probably having stayed upstairs to hang out with Monica in the choreography lounge. She *loves* those two, constantly trying out new steps and trading secrets, like she's one of the kids. It's infuriating: *I'm* not even one of the kids, and I'm literally one of the kids.

"You wish Monica would invite you into the cool

club, huh?" Asella says. Apparently I'm staring at Hollie and Keith. Especially Keith.

"Oh. You noticed?"

"Listen. Some kids rely on natural talent," she says, popping her chin at the two wonder-teens. "And *some* kids"—here, she whomps me across the shoulder—"work their buns off for a scrap of glory."

Not fast enough. My buns have actually gotten buns-ier since getting to New York. All those street hot dogs. "You said there was a trade. So let's say I do the event . . ."

"I need something from you, Nate."

"Anything," I want to shout. But I recall this one time when Libby negotiated a lower pizza price after Papa John's ran out of mushrooms, and so I just go: "I'm *listening*."

"Kid, I can't keep up with all these script changes."

Asella drops her bookbag, zipping open the top chamber. Sure enough, behind an entire pineapple and a jar of travel-size Metamucil, Asella's binder is spilling pages like a murderee's guts.

"Listen, I've been away from the theater for ten years. Thank God for guest spots on *Law & Order*, may it rest in peace."

Man, would I love to be on TV! *Nate: The TV Experience,* in 3-D even. Unless my zits would overwhelm viewers.

"And on TV, you get one take down and the director yells, 'cut,' and you never have to remember the lines again."

The nameless guardian zooms past us in the lobby, trailing after Keith and Hollie. "Nate, we couldn't find you upstairs. Are you taking him out to lunch, Asella?"

"Sure," Asella says, flashing the fake dummy-smile of a ventriloquist act. "I adore kids."

The door slams and she turns back to me, her smile disintegrating like a box of Cracker Jacks around yours truly.

"Listen," she says. "Every lunch break. You and me. Till previews start. I need a scene partner, somebody to run the E.T. lines with me so I'm up to speed. At any moment, I could have to fill in for Mackey." She shivers at the thought.

This is unreal. Asella sounds just the way I did when I first begged Libby to coach me in acting. I'd seen Libby, then a brand-new student to my school, bribe her way out of a History test, claiming the phrase "French and Indian War" was so racially insensitive, she was feeling light-headed. And I remember thinking: I need to know this girl.

"So you want me to just . . . read the other parts?" I say. "Opposite E.T.?"

"Sure. I've watched you in those rehearsals up

there, Nate. You're always beating yourself up. You're always taking the blame. I like that in a scene partner."

This might be the nicest thing said about me in ages—ever since I got a C-minus in Spanish and the teacher wrote: *Believe it or not, Nate is my favorite student* on my report card. She was the rare adult who appreciated a well-placed *Seussical* reference.

"Besides, you might learn a thing or two from me," Asella says, straightening her glasses. "We *do* both cover E.T."

"Even if they'll never put me on."

"Listen. Let's not overthink this. I need someone to drill me on my dialogue." She changes strategies, beginning to kind of shout. "And I've got a very elderly dachshund at home." The security guard stands up. "And my husband would've run lines with me if he hadn't run *off* with another lady. *Is that what you've been waiting for me to say, kid?*"

Her eyes flick to the guard.

"No!" I yell. "No, I didn't think old wiener dogs would come up today at all." This makes me suddenly hungry, again, for a hot dog or three. My caloric kryptonite.

"Great," Asella says, instantly calm. "Every lunch, then. From now until official understudy rehearsals start. *Your* job is just to make sure I'm not just making up my own lines." She suddenly seems grown-up-nervous and not middle-school-nervous.

"I'm just—wow." I clear my throat. "Why me? You could ask anyone to run lines with you." Like an adult. Like somebody with experience and a voice that knows its own octave.

Asella lifts her bag. "You wanna do the event with Jordan on TV? And sneak under the radar in my place?"

"I do." Terribly, I do. Besides the glamour, it's half a paycheck. Someone I love could use that cash. Maybe even me. (I've still gotta pay for my opening night tux.)

"Then I don't think it's about how badly I need *you*," she says. "I think it's about how badly you need me."

She turns and kicks the door to Forty-second Street open.

"Where are you going?" I say against a whooshing wind.

"To a major appointment."

"Is this our first date?" My voice cracks, again. Which is officially becoming a "thing."

"Tomorrow. We start tomorrow. Today I'm having a mani-pedi, and I can't imagine you'd want one of those."

I look at my hands: fingernails gnawed to the cuticle, knuckles dry as all get-out, palms beat up where I scratched them on Heidi's fire escape. My hands *look* like E.T.'s.

"Oh, come *on*," Asella says, tugging me by the jacket sleeve. "There's a two-for-one special at a Korean place off Sixth. We can get a jump start on these scenes while they're scrubbing our feet."

"I don't let people touch my feet," I'm attempting to relay, but Asella is four entire regular-size people lengths ahead of me, leading me through Times Square.

I'm off to my first mani-pedi.

And into my first grown-up trade.

Koreaaaah Spaaaaaah

(Two weeks and six days till first preview)

First things first. You can't be shy about your feet when you go to a Korean nail spa.

"Oh, you don't have to do that," I say to the very nice woman who's throwing my shoes into a corner of the store. And now going for a sock.

"Oh, yes she does," Asella says, putting her *Us* magazine down and taking a sip of tea. "I'm paying for the whole kaboodle. We're getting the whole kaboodle."

"But I'm ticklish."

"Grow up," she says, flipping to "Who Wore It Best."

It's quite a sight, here: We've got our feet in bowls of hot water, and I'm sitting in a padded vinyl chair, but Asella's legs can't reach from the seat, so she's just kind of standing up. It's actually adorable.

"Well, if we're here, we should work," I say, trying not to flinch as this spa lady basically does everything but put a feather to my foot.

"Good," Asella says, placing the magazine in a

rack and pulling out her script. I pop a few ginger candies, confiscated on our way in. "I suppose we should've gotten you lunch," she says, watching me.

"Oh, I'll be fine." My tongue is burning off.

"So, should we start with E.T. and Elliott's first scene?" Asella says. At least I think she does. I'm distracted by this beauty technician lady tearing away at my feet with what appears to be sandpaper. (I always skipped Woodshop class back home, so I might not have my terminology straight.)

"Okay," I say through a mouth piping with lava-hot ginger. "So the first time E.T. talks—let's start there. I'll read Elliott and Gertie."

"How about that *Genna*?" Asella says. "Somebody ought to sew her mouth shut and sell her on eBay."

This would make me laugh if Genna weren't my only (secret) fan. I gesture to Asella's script: "So, we're *reading*."

"Where's *your* script?" Asella says, examining a wet toe.

I point to my head. "All up here," I say, plowing into Elliott's first line: *"If there's something secret I wanted to show you, wouldja promise not to tell Mom?"* I switch gears, doing a Genna impersonation: *"What kind of a secret?"*

"Skipping ahead," Asella goes. She knows E.T. doesn't enter for another page.

"I was just setting the mood!"

"Unless you're buying me dinner and paying for Doc's irritable bowel meds, don't bother with *mood*."

"Doc?"

"My dog," Asella says, taking a gulp of her newly refilled tea, her glasses fogging.

"Right. Okay. So, skipping ahead. Page twenty-five, I think? Starting with Elliott." I close my eyes and channel Jordan. *"Do you like 'em, boy?"*

Here, I pretend to hand Asella the Reese's Pieces, using a "Koreaaaah Spaaaaaah" pamphlet as a prop.

"We're doing *blocking*?" Asella says, taking the brochure and flicking it into the trash.

"Well, yeah. You might as well put the lines with the staging."

"Elliott and his alien pet are not getting a mani-pedi onstage, my dear." She's got a point, though I'm not sure why she's being so much trouble. "Besides, you're intimidating me. I barely know the lines and you've got the *moves* down."

It's true. I can watch anything once and get it, unless it involves climbing the rope in gym.

"Whatever," I say, watching as the nice Korean woman takes my favorite hand (left) and douses it with this superchilly glue stuff. "When you're not in many scenes, what else is there to do but watch the stars rehearse?"

"Chin up," Asella says, so I do. "Not literally, Nate. Jesus."

"Oh, right."

"Okay. You've handed me the Reeses Pieces," she says. "*Onstage*. Not here."

"*Do you like 'em, boy?*" I say again, back to Elliott's lines.

"*Blip blip schwimmmmmm,*" Asella says.

But she doesn't exactly say it.

She turns her voice into a mechanical airplane bouncing from the walls, ringing out in a high-pitch, otherworldly trill that causes the salon worker to drop my hand and look around, as if the spa's being robbed by aliens.

"That is *amazing*," I say. "How you do that?"

"Is that Elliott's new line?" Asella hollers, water splashing. "Did they change his line again?" She flips through her script in a panic.

"No. No. The *voice* thing."

The Korean lady takes my hand and stares at it wondrously, like perhaps *it* made the noise, sent from a distant land with an important message.

"I did a lot of cartoons with this voice," Asella says, hacking up a glob of phlegm. "The trick is to place all the noise in your nose. Pretend you're going to sneeze and then talk."

"Cool." I try it and just end up sneezing. On my manicurist. "Sorry."

"Keep practicing. Back to the lines?"

"Yes, yes," I say, taking Asella's script so she can't

cheat. *"Be careful, now. Don't eat 'em all. Could give you a bellyache you'd never recover from."*

Jordan's actually pretty good on that line. He plays it like E.T. is about to *die* or something, but he really pulls it off. I hate him for this.

"Now, is this where I do another *blip blip* whatever," Asella says, "or where I go *bloop blop.*"

"It's *Gwim gwom gurrrrr,*" I say, staring at my fingers as they're attacked with clippers. (I sliced into Feather's quick once, when I was trimming his nails, and he bled for about a week. I'm not sure if humans have the same parts, but I'm basically sitting so still, my hamstring starts to cramp.)

"Right," Asella says, chewing a lip. *"Gwim gwom gurrrrr."*

"I mean . . . honestly?" I say, finally breathing as the lady drops my hand to get Asella another tea. "Can't you just sort of make up the noises between Elliott's lines? They're all nonsense sounds anyway."

Asella takes my forearm with such startling strength that I yelp. "No, Nate. *No.*" She hops out of the water bowl, dripping onto my little pile of socks. "We have to respect what the writer writes."

But wait! *"You* were giving Dewey a hard time about the word *fly,* back in the rehearsal room. Right before my voice committed category six suicide."

Asella drops my arm, takes a swig of new tea, and

considers. "Yes, well. I suppose I like to boss Dewey. He's fun to push around."

"How do you mean?"

"Oh, you know. I woulda had my big *comeback* if it weren't for his loyalty to Mackey." Asella steps back into her bowl. "And *somebody's* gotta challenge Dewey's vision, or we're going to end up in a live-action video game bomb."

"I thought his last project sold, like, a billion zillion dollars."

"Dewey's last project was for teenage boys. Do you know how many teenage boys go see musicals?"

If they're anything like me, a billion zillion. "None," I say. Because they're not anything like me.

"Anyway," Asella says, "I need to pick my nail polish, and then *we* need to head back to the studio." Asella towels off her feet and pulls out a couple of twenties. From her bra, by the way. "This was a good warm-up for our next session, kid. You're on it. I'm impressed."

"Can I contribute anything to this?"

"You already have." She pays our ladies. "Come here. Do boys wear nail polish these days? According to the news, anything goes."

"No way," I say, examining my hands. They look pretty good: puffy and pink, like—*yum*—Canadian bacon.

"Your stomach's growling."

"I'm not sure the ginger candy is going to hold me."

We skip the polish and take off for rehearsal, with Asella waddling ahead of me on the street. "I'm buying you a Balance Bar or something," she says, running into a bodega and right back out again, like a magician.

"Did you *steal* that?" I say, opening my least favorite flavor, but happy all the same.

"No," she says, taking off again, "they know me there. I used to walk the owner's pit bull, but there was an incident with my Doc. Free Balance Bars for life, is all I'm saying."

This lady's tricky.

We get past the security guard, flashing our badges (every time!) and heading to the elevator, when he stops us. "Wait. You're Nathan Foster, yeah?"

"Look at you," Asella says, "a celeb."

"You've got a package here."

I sidestep to the guard's desk.

"We've got approximately not-even-one minute till rehearsal starts," Asella says, holding the elevator as the buzzer starts. "Get a move on."

The security guard tosses me a giant see-through garbage bag—weighed down with a toy.

"Oh my God."

I reach for my Nokia, dialing Mom's number at work. And just as I'm about to bawl her out—how could she send Libby's teddy bear to *me*? And why on earth did she put it in a *pirate's* costume, anyway?—a text buzzes in.

"ur unreal."

From Libby.

"perfect timing. mom got some good news today AND the teddy bear of all time just arrived. luv you natey."

"Let's go, kid," Asella says.

My feet walk to the elevator, perhaps even taking the rest of me along. I'm not paying any attention. I'm digging open the new package, looking a little closer at the bear. This didn't come from my mom's shop. It smells too good, like freshness and affection and not guilt and unpaid taxes. And that's when I notice the tag: *Getting closer to guessing who I am?*

"You asked me if boys wear nail polish," I say to Asella, who's suddenly knifing open a mango, right here in the elevator.

"Yup?" she goes.

"They don't. They get teddy bears from girls who wear too much nail polish."

"The type of girls who should be sold on eBay?" Asella says, her face contorting into all-out disgust.

"Bull's-eye," I say, stuffing the pirate bear into my bookbag, the elevator doors parting for our afternoon rehearsal.

"Hey, Nate?"

"Yeah?" I say, zipping the bookbag shut and leading Asella to the sign-in sheet.

"Don't tell anyone we're running lines." She goes from zero to vulnerable in two seconds—and for the first time seems as small as she really is. "I can't have the creative team thinking . . . I can't hack it."

"Hack what?" Monica says, suddenly next to us by the corkboard.

Asella's caught off-guard.

"This mango," I say, grabbing it from her. Its mysterious juice gushes all over my plump new hands. "She can't hack this *mango. You* know mangoes." God, Nate. "And stuff."

Before Monica can even react, Roscoe shouts, "Actors, we are *back* from lunch and *tapping* in one minute!"

And Asella takes my perfect puffy hand and gives it a secret squeeze.

William O'Keefe

(Two weeks till first preview)

Heidi runs out to the twenty-four-hour Duane Reade to pick up "lady things" (I don't ask), and I'm done with my homework, so I look for Libby online. She's there in one Skype click.

"My Quixote."

"My windmill."

She's lounging on her bed, painting her nails. Libby never paints her nails. "You never paint your nails. Since when did you start painting your nails?"

"Since my best friend left me for a life of fame-dom."

Fame-dom! "Ha! Libby, most of my days are spent trying not to get cut from production numbers."

She caps the polish, grabs a foot, and blows on her toes. Neither of us is flexible, so it's pretty impressive; she looks like Gumby after a car accident. "Well, whatever. By the time you're back in Jankburg, I'm going to be painting more than my nails."

I minimize my own face onscreen. "Oh?"

"Yes. I'm going to be painting the white picket fence on the house I will own—with my first potential ex-husband."

I give her the WTF eyebrow.

"William O'Keefe," she says. Really slow.

"William 'Bill' O'Keefe?" I say, maximizing the face window to see what I look like when I'm this surprised. Or hurt. "He *torments* me, Libby."

"*Tormented.* Past tense, Natey."

"He T.P.'d my mom's minivan, Libby. *While I was in it.*"

"Not true. James Madison did. Bill just stood guard. And ever since James was expelled for the firecracker incident, the Bills have lightened up *considerably.*"

James Madison and his Bills of Rights, the most notorious bullies in a school of fish packed to the *gills* with future criminals, were the worst of the worst. They hated me for loving musicals. They hated me for being friends with girls. They hated my clothes (so did I), my accent (I adopted something vaguely French during seventh grade), they even hated my dog (having once stumbled upon me and Feather acting out a scene from *Into the Woods* in the forest behind our house).

"I'm just . . . surprised, is all."

But I'm more than surprised. Bill O'Keefe used to hold my bookbag while James Madison gave me Indian rug burns.

"Here's the deal," Libby says, grabbing the teddy bear from Mom's shop and clutching it like a toddler. My own pirate bear sits at my feet.

"Don't pull the innocent kid act on me, Libby."

I hear Heidi's front door open, and she races for the bathroom. Perhaps her "lady things" will keep her busy for a while longer.

I continue. "That teddy bear"—besides being superexpensive—"shouldn't be, like, a bargaining tool here. I mean . . . Bill O'Keefe, Libby? *Seriously*?"

"Nate, what do you *expect*? I'm getting older. And Billy was directionless without James."

"So . . . what?" I say, hearing my voice getting madder. "You swooped in and rescued him? Have you also put *him* on a diet?"

Bill O'Keefe is the exact shape of the first letter of his last name.

"Watch it, Nate," Libby says, casting the teddy bear aside. "There's nothing wrong with Billy having a little more to love. *You* should know."

Sting. Also, Libby and I have the same silhouette, so she's basically just making fun of herself.

"You're obviously mad at me for something," I

want to dare myself to say. But I hate confrontation. She's my best friend in the world, ever and forever. Maybe this is just a stage. Maybe she's just jealous of me.

"There's a girl in the show who's into *me*, actually," I say. "She's acting a lot like *you're* acting. All swoony over *Billy*. So maybe she's serious about it."

I start playing with a paperweight on Heidi's desk, fascinated people still have such things.

"You don't say," Libby goes.

"I do say. This girl keeps leaving me stuff."

"What kind of stuff?" Libby's eyebrows knit.

"Drawings. Teddy bears. Candy."

Genna hasn't left me candy, yet, but it's bound to happen. Besides, you always deliver a list in threes. (See: Stooges.)

"So lemme get this . . . *straight*," Libby says, standing and blowing a bubble. "Once you send somebody a teddy bear, you're declaring an act of *romance*?" She picks up her own gift, holding it by the ear like it's a smoking pistol.

"Something like that," I say. "But look. We're different."

"Yes, we are. *You* are."

"Whatever." I plop the paperweight down and Heidi's desk rattles. From a crack in her window, a wave of cold air hisses like a haunted ambulance.

"We're all changing. You're painting your nails now that you've got a boyfriend. I get it."

"Speaking of nails," Libby says, pulling her laptop closer and unhinging her jaw in mock shock. "Did you have *your* nails done?"

"*Kind* of," I say, examining them closer—and thrilled to get away from the last subject. "You could see them all the way in Jankburg? They're not even painted."

"Nah," Libby says. "But you're not biting them like normal. So I assume you treated yourself to a day spa or something."

Nothing gets by Libby. She's like Nancy Drew on Ritalin.

"Do you *like* the teddy bear?" I manage, finally.

"Should Karen Morrow have won the Tony for *I Had A Ball*?" This one's obscure for even me, but I know what Libby means. Of course she loves the teddy bear. "Listen . . . I have a secret." Her eyes suddenly dart.

"Oh no," I say. "Mom-stuff?"

"No, Mom-stuff's on the upswing. She didn't puke at all this week."

Yikes. "That's an upswing?"

"That's an upswing."

"Got it."

Libby holds up my green rabbit foot. "I've been

praying on this sucker. Seems to be working."

Heidi ducks her head in the door. "Hello to your friend and then gotta get ready for bed, Natey."

"Aunts," I whisper to Libby.

"Please. You live the coolest life, Nate."

I guess it is pretty cool. I guess it is pretty *cold*. A kid can practically see his own breath in Heidi's apartment, but I don't want to hurt her feelings and insult her window insulation or anything. Dad used to work in insulation, before becoming a janitor at the hospital, so we've got an old-as-heck house but it's warm-as-heck, too. Call it Dad's biggest triumph.

"So what kind of secret are we talking about, here, Lib?"

"Okay. So. Remember how they found a male porno magazine in Little Bill's locker?"

"Vaguely," I say.

Specifically, actually. After a famous school-bathroom firecracker incident over Halloween, James's and the Bills' lockers were searched. All Libby's new boyfriend's turned up was an unsurprising motherload of Entenmann's products. But the *other* Bill's locker was more . . . revealing.

"So it turns out James Madison definitely *did not* plant the magazine," Libby says.

"Why are you so certain?" I say too fast.

Thing is, James Madison is just the type of criminal mastermind to try to frame a co-bully. Libby has all the *Sopranos* seasons on Blu-ray, so I know a lot about this kind of stuff.

"Because James is so disgusted by the gays, he swears he'd never even *touch* that magazine."

"Tell me you're not talking to James, Libby."

She uncaps a Diet Mountain Dew—withdrawn, mysteriously, from beneath a pillow—and shrugs. "I'm not, personally. No. But Billy is."

I sigh so deeply, I practically fall from Heidi's chair. "Okay, okay," I say, hearing myself getting a little too worked up over this news. "So what's your *secret*?"

"The *secret* is that the other Bill—Little Bill—is definitely gay."

I make myself count to three before picking up a magazine on Heidi's dresser, flipping it open to a random page. "Oh," I say, in a supercasual way. I play it so cool I'm practically doing an impression of the weather.

Libby grunts. "Yes. His mom signed him up for tap class and everything."

"Oh yeah?" I turn a page and manage a pretty convincing fake yawn.

"Give it up, Nate. Your magazine's upside down."

Drat. I toss it to the floor.

"Okay," I say. "I'll bite. What makes you so sure the other Bill is . . . like . . . *that*."

"*Gay*? Because he switched his Facebook profile

from Conservative to Liberal," Libby says, swigging at the Diet Dew, "and added *What Ever Happened to Baby Jane?* to his favorite movies."

"So?"

"Don't be an amateur, Nate," she says, tossing the dead Dew into the trash and pulling out a bag of light pretzels. "People always come out in stages. He's testing the waters." She sits up straight. "And *that* has inspired me—here's the secret!—to start a Gay-Straight Alliance at school. I want Little Bill and *my* Billy on the steering committee."

"Cool." I've run out of things to play with on Heidi's desk. "I should go in a sec. Uh . . . Aunt's getting antsy and all that."

On perfect cue, Heidi shouts "Lights out, you two" from the living room.

"So . . . *Any* thoughts on what I should *call* the GSA?" Libby says.

"Wow. You haven't been this riled up since you won tickets to see Linda Eder at Heinz Hall."

"Well," Libby says, polishing off the pretzels four at a time. "It's nice to be 'about' something, you know?"

I do know. I used to think the only thing I was about was being the only boy who liked musicals. And now that I'm around so many of them—now that I'm far from the home I love (*Fiddler* ballad reference)—I don't know what I'm about anymore.

"I'm . . . I feel confused, too," I say. "About something."

"You can say it, Natey," Libby says, her voice bursting. She takes off her glasses and gives me a look so earnest, it practically shatters Heidi's computer screen.

"I'm confused by how many diet products you're consuming."

"Oh, screw *off*, Foster," Libby says, slumping back into her bed's hundred pillows.

"I'm *serious!* When I get home, I'm not putting up with Diet Dew."

"That implies you're coming home at all," she says, frowning.

"Well, if you want a preview of me in the meantime . . . if you want to see me on national television, in HD . . ."

"And you know I do!" she says, bolting to her feet.

"Do not tell *anyone*, but I've got a big appearance coming up. The day before previews start. It's a surprise."

"*Nate!*" she screams. "Why didn't you say something earlier? What is it? Like a live-broadcast dinner with the mayor or something? On top of the Chrysler Building?"

"Ha-ha," I say, standing to kick off my sneakers. "Nothing like that."

And why *didn't* I say something earlier? Maybe because I can only have one secret at a time, with one girl at a time. It's weird to say, but Asella's like the grown-up version of Libby. And maybe I'm just a one-lady-at-a-time kind of guy.

"I'm just not allowed to say anything more about it."

"Well—*ugh*," Libby says. "Okay. Wow. I'll mark my calendar, sport." She starts clapping. "And promise not to tell anyone."

"Not *even* Bill 'the boyfriend' O'Keefe," I say.

"Oh, he wouldn't listen, anyway," she says, waving me away. "He couldn't care less about Broadway."

There's a big pause here, and maybe I'm imagining it but I'm pretty sure Scram leaves the room just because it's so awkward.

"Well, sounds like Bill's pretty great, Libby," I say, grinding molars.

"He is," she says. "Or . . . he's not. But he's something. I've never had a something."

"You had me."

"*Libby.*" Her mom knocks on her door. Libby's never in trouble. I wouldn't be surprised if Mrs. Jones was just delivering Libby another box of Dew. Or, sorry: *Diet* Dew.

"I'm gonna jet, Lib."

"Me too, Greaty. Hey, Greaty?"

"Yup."

"How's the world of understudying coming?"

"Oh. She's fantastic."

"*She's* fantastic? You're referring to yourself in the third person feminine and you're surprised *I'm* starting a Gay-Straight Alliance?"

God. "No. The E.T. understudy. The first one. I've been coaching her for a week."

"*What?* You should be . . . pushing her down *stairs.*"

Asella would roll. Man, that would be a sight. "Remember all those times you drilled me on scenes? Taught me how to react better? Broke down how to breathe while singing?"

"*Remember?*" Libby says. "I'm still waiting to get paid."

"Well, I'm using those lessons now. I'm . . . helping Asella run lines."

"Kid of the year, Natey," Libby says, finally seeming like her old self. "Kid of the year after *moi.*"

"*Libby,* honey," I hear Mrs. Jones say.

"The mothership."

"Man your station," I say, and then, "I really miss you."

But she's already logged off. And even though she usually leaves me smiling or laughing, tonight Libby just leaves behind a cloud of questions.

And now it's just me and my cold toes in a cold room where the only warm thing is my nervous breath. Wondering what this *What Ever Happened to Baby Jane?* is all about.

And if Little Bill is watching it, right now.

Dressing Rooms and Prunes

(One week till first preview)

We're all thinking it so allow me to verbalize it: You haven't lived until you've walked through a stage door. To say I've dreamed of this moment is the understatement of my short but endless life (see: the Jankburg Era).

"Okay, boys, you're all on floor three." But by the time Kiana the stage manager is yelling, "Walk, don't run," it's too late. We're tearing up the stairs, four at a time, giggling and screaming and hurling toward our dressing room.

"I'll be right there, guys."

Let me make a small correction. I'm just giggling. *They're* giggling and screaming and hurling. Keith (soul singer, Jordan's understudy), Robbie (veteran of four Broadway shows, the kind of kid who falls out of bed into the full splits), and Nick (a model whose face has graced the covers of all my favorite issues of "Pottery Barn Kids")—*they're* pushing their way up the stairwell.

It's our first day in the theater. I'm taking it slow, admiring the banister, thinking about all the shows that have played here. It's outrageous. *The dancers from* A Chorus Line *walked these steps, guys.*

"Hello, *Nate*."

"Oh—hi, *Genna*."

She's holding one of those hair-straightener appliances Libby's got back home, but Genna's looks about fifty times more expensive. And a hundred times more pink.

"How's your dressing room?" she says, bopping the iron against her thigh. I'm probably making her supernervous.

"Oh, I don't know yet. At all." Or maybe *I'm* just nervous. Nobody's ever had a crush on me. "Haven't been up there. To the rooms. The dressing rooms." Smooth, Nate.

"Well, the leads are about to have a little sparkling-apple-cider toast in *my* dressing room. To celebrate day one in the theater."

"Cool!"

"Feel free to stop by, if you pass our floor. Invite only."

I'm about to ask if I can bring Keith—apple juice is his favorite drink, not that I know everything about him—when Genna gets pulled away by the girls.

"Are you coming or what, Nate?" Robbie yells from upstairs. (He has a habit of yelling because of a mild hearing issue, actually.) "You're going to miss out on claiming a spot in the dressing room."

But you know what? "One sec, Robbie." When you've had a whole life of getting picked last, you end up playing into it. I'll never be fastest. I'll never be first, and when you realize you'll never be first, the best thing you can do is set yourself up to be last. That way you're the most at *something*. The ultimate. The pinnacle or the least. I'd rather hang out in the hallway. I'd rather be on the end than in the middle. When you're on "the end," you're always closer to the metaphorical bathroom, anyway.

"Too late," Keith says, bouncing a ball against the mirrors in our magnificent, hospital-white dressing room, "your spot's by the bathroom."

"I don't mind," I say. I don't mind at all. I'm backstage on Broadway with three other boys my age, and they're not even making fun of me for it. Besides, this way I can dash into the bathroom to change my costumes.

"We should, like, decorate our room!" Robbie says. "What kind of theme should we do it in?" (He's screaming.)

"Hawaii is really cool," Nick offers. "I shot an

'Abercrombie Kids' catalog in Hawaii and it's a really soothing place."

"Soothing?" Keith says, snorting. "Ha-ha-ha, *soothing*. That's hilarious, man. 'Welcome to our dressing room. We hope you feel 'soothied.'"

"*Soothed*," I'm about to correct, but I'd never take Keith down. And anyway, I'm more drawn to a note card on my makeup table. "Did one of you guys put this here?"

I have my own makeup table, if you missed that.

"Nope," Keith says, tossing his ball hard enough for our mirror to rattle. "Sorry, y'all," he says. "I bet my ball bouncing isn't *soothing*."

Everyone cracks up and Nick says a bad word, but I'm too busy opening the envelope to engage in this nonsense. Willingly, at least. Apparently ignoring Keith's brilliant joke sets him off, because I am suddenly in a headlock.

"Hey! Cut it out!" I promise myself to yell—just as soon as I figure out why I don't mind Keith putting me into a headlock.

"Is the *kid* in here?" we hear, and the four of us flip our heads to see Asella, holding a rolling suitcase and a birdcage, surrounded by a flood of boxes.

"Whoa," Keith says, letting me go. I fall into the wall and frankly don't mind being smashed back to earth. "You moving in, Asella?"

"You bet," she says. "*Yeah*, it's bad luck getting too comfortable when you don't even know if the show'll run, but I've got my requirements." She kicks a box. "And I need a hand."

Nick goes to help—for a model, he's really helpful—but Asella puts her teeny palm out. "Not you," she says. Ninety bucks she has no idea what his name is. No idea what *any* of their names are. "The kid."

"We're all kids," Robbie shouts from on high, tiptoeing atop his chair to inspect a ceiling speaker.

"I'm no kid," Keith says, catapulting the ball at Robbie. "I shaved five weeks ago."

The ball ricochets off Robbie's back and nails Asella square in the chin. She barely flinches, catching it on the next bounce and tossing it into one of her boxes.

"People who shave should move beyond toys," she says, turning to the stairs. "You *helping* me, or what?"

I head to the door, cramming the unread note card into my back pocket.

"You're 'the kid'?" Nick says.

"I'm 'the kid,'" I go, suddenly aware how uncool it is to have a friend in her fifties—and also, that we've kept our friendship totally quiet. Still, our weekly mani-pedis have become a Nathan Foster life necessity.

"Well, are you going to stand there or are you

going to lift something?" Asella says. I guess I'm staring at a thousand signatures scrawled across the hallway ceiling.

"That's *amazing*," I say, pointing to the autographs.

"That's *depressing*," Asella says, pulling a box of prunes from thin air. "You only sign that ceiling when your show *closes*, kid." She picks up a crate. "It's like—I dunno. Do people still sign yearbooks?"

She says *yearbooks* like it's a swearword, her face folded into itself.

"Yes, people sign yearbooks—though they're fifty dollars, so Libby and I share one."

Asella follows me upstairs to the adult dressing rooms. "Who's this Libby character supposed to be?"

"Libby?" Saying her name out loud . . . it's like I'm a sponge and Libby's the first drop of water in forever. "She's my best friend."

"She's your Doc, huh?"

"My faithful dachshund?"

"No other kind," Asella goes, kicking her dressing room door open and plopping a box down at her spot. I pull out my phone to text Libby: "ur my faithful doxen." She'll like that.

"Okay," Asella says, flipping the lights on and rerouting to business mode. "I'm sharing this dressing room with that Amazon warrior-girl, April, so I'd like to be very clear about which half is mine."

She pulls out a roll of bright green tape.

"That stuff is incredible!" I say. "Did you get that at Duane Reade?" Duane Reade is a store in New York that sells everything under the sun except, like, airplane parts and pets.

"No," Asella says, ripping off an expanse of tape and palming it straight across the middle of their shared table. She's drawing a border. Enemy lines. "No, this is the tape stage management uses to mark out the floor." She sighs, knowing everything's bound to be a lesson when your closest companion is a middle schooler. "You know what a *spike* mark is, yes?"

"Of course," I say, "I was *born* knowing that." Though I actually just learned the term two weeks ago, when a stage manager *spiked* the outline of the fake tree that Garret Charles has me standing behind for the *entire opening number*. "Well, that's cool," I say, shaking off the memory. "That stage management loaned you that fancy tape."

"Loaned?" Asella says. "Please, kid. The key to life is to take what you want and ask for forgiveness later."

Suddenly I wonder if that Balance Bar a few weeks ago was, in fact, stolen.

"By the by," Asella says, rooting through her purse. "Sorry to pull you away from your gang downstairs."

"No big thing," I say.

"It's just nice to see you chorus kids chumming it

up. Since the *stars* certainly won't give us the time of day."

I'm not so sure about that! *"Actually,"* I say, breaking into a whisper, "Genna won't quit it with the secret admirer gifts. And she invited me to a drink reception that I am *currently* missing. So . . . stars, you know? They're just like us!"

Asella doesn't laugh. "I hate to break it to you," she says instead, removing a lone, sad hanger from a rack, "but that Genna must be two-timing you. She's so openly hot for Jordan Rylance, it's practically illegal watching her play his younger sister."

What? "What are you talki—"

"Listen. Genna's got a crush on Jordan so bad, Dewey calls her Genna Rylance. The whole company knows. Where's your head been?"

In the sky. Looking at autographs. Thinking about Keith. And Little Bill. (And . . . Jordan.)

"Then what's with these notes she's giving me?" I say to Asella, suddenly remembering the envelope that's hiding in my pocket. I rip into it, eager to share the evidence that an actual girl likes an actual Nate.

"Get to my dressing room before rehearsal starts." But it's not from Genna, this time. *"I've got a headline."*

"This is from . . . you," I say.

Asella curtsies.

"Weird." I try to shake it off, but . . . Genna's got

two crushes? Is this what cheating feels like? "So . . . what's your headline, Asella?"

"Actors," we hear over the backstage monitor, *"start getting into microphones. We'll do a tour of the theater and then begin spacing the dance break in 'Long-Necked Neighbor from Outa' Space.'"*

"So here's the deal," she says. I didn't know a deal was being made. "The event, with Jordan?"

"There's *more* to this deal?" I say, letting her suitcase drop to the floor.

"It's nothing big," Asella says, "but Monica and Garret added some staging. To the song. Just for the event. I had a last-minute rehearsal yesterday. And before I forget everything they showed me, I need to show y—"

"Is it complicated?" My stomach boils and freezes at the same time.

"Relax, kid," she says. She hasn't called me Nate once today. She might *actually* think my name is Kid Foster. "There's a little, like, waltzy thing that happens in the middle of Jordan's big song. The one *you'll* be co-starring in."

"On TV," I remind her, the universe, myself.

"Right. And *I* picked up the sequence fine, but I've seen you dance." Asella stops, trying to find words that won't flatten me. "It might take you a smidge more time to pick up. And we've only got less than a week."

"What are you saying?" I'm counting on this money. I'm counting on being on TV. I don't even *like* counting. (See: my math tests.)

"If you want to pull off this event, I have to teach you the steps."

"Okay. Okay. Can we—I don't know. Do we have *time*?"

"We'll have to make the time. On five-minute breaks, during lunch, at night."

"My Aunt Heidi will never let me stay in midtown after rehearsal."

"It's your tail, kid," Asella says, biting off a hunk of tape and hooking the roll to a clip on her belt. The room looks like a neon crime scene, like somebody taped out the body of a dead hexagon.

"We'll do it, then," I say. "We have to. I can't go on national TV and not know the staging."

"That's the attitude, kid," she says, thrusting that box of prunes at me. "Go for it."

I take a handful in my mouth. It's like if slugs were covered in Splenda, these "prunes."

"Good," Asella says, closing up the box and pulling out a humidifier. "Close the door," she says. "We've got five minutes until the backstage tour starts, and we need to steam our throats."

"Screw our throats," I say, kneeing the door shut. "Let's start waltzing."

"Attaboy. Start on the left foot." She stares me down and talks superslow. "You'll hold for three counts of eight after Jordan finishes the first chorus of his song."

"Oh God. This already sounds like Geometry," I say—still figuring out how not to swallow these prunes, now wedged between two teeth.

"You can do it." She holds out a garbage can, I spit out the prunes, and we start again—right after she says, "I believe in you, Nate."

The Nearly Main Event Almost

One thing when you're going to be on live national television for the first time is that you shouldn't eat a lot the night before. Free tip!

I'm already gurgly, the fear of screwing up in front of millions of viewers bopping through my head like a bad summer song. And on top of that, last night was Breakfast for Dinner at Aunt Heidi's, and she's actually pretty expert at French toast. Which means I had three helpings just to make sure.

"You look a little . . . white," the chef in question says, nudging my knee on the subway ride into the city.

"My skin hasn't seen the sun in months," I say. "I'm like the veal of middle school."

Aunt Heidi laughs, but it's true: My skin is so see-through, you can make out veins.

"I still can't believe," she says, sipping from a tremendous thermos of coffee, "the producers didn't send a private car for you." I should note that Heidi has begun making coffee at home in the mornings. She just quit her waitress job to focus on acting, so she's become "quite frugal"—which means "poor" in Latin. "I just can't believe the star of the number has to take the *seven* train. Who do I have to talk to about this?"

This wakes me up. "Nobody! You don't have to say a word!"

The whole scenario today is risky, bordering on death. Heidi's not in on the big secret switcheroo— only Asella, the stage manager, and me. And Libby. And my dreams.

"You know," I say, punting, "E.T. had to come to America in a big metal tube, himself. So it's like . . . I'm getting in character. On the subway. And stuff." My lies are less clear at dawn. Man, it's early out.

"Okay, sport. Whatever you say. Next stop is ours."

Thank God Asella worked out today's scheme with Roscoe; he's going to pick me up on a very specific corner—a few blocks from the event in Central Park—and get me into costume before anyone (named Jordan Rylance) catches wise. Roscoe's cool that way, if you don't mind your adults pulling fast ones on other kids.

"Look alive, Nate." Heidi and I shuffle out and push upstairs to the street level.

Problem is, fast things don't usually go so hot for yours sincerely.

"Don't blow your breath like it's cigarette smoke," Heidi says. We're power walking in the icy air to Columbus Circle. "I'm thirty-four days into quitting and I don't need the reminder."

Just then a pack of noisy teenagers, who look like they never went home last night, walks by us, each possessing a cigarette and a haircut they'll regret if anyone has a camera.

"Look *away*, Aunt Heidi," I say. "Look *awaaaay!*"

But she doesn't even see them. "Heads up," she says, instead, "it's that *Jordan* boy—"

Bundled up from cowlick to Converse, in a plush, luxurious sleeping bag of a jacket: Jordan Rylance steps out of a (private) car, his Mommy following just after, enveloped in her signature leopard coat. Her gloved hand clutches an egg and cheese sandwich, which steams like a volcano.

"—and his *mother*," Heidi mutters.

All four of us met at the audition, and Heidi's no big fan of Mrs. Rylance. That said, I bet the biggest fan of Mrs. Rylance is some jeweler in Western Pennsylvania. The lady sparkles like the Big Dipper. Good nickname for her too, since my mood essentially takes a crashing dip whenever she's within twenty feet.

"Okay, Aunt Heidi," I say, flipping around to cover

my face and practically pulling my T-shirt up and over my head. "Guess you can drop me off now!"

"What are you *talking* about?" she says. "I'm gonna stand in the crowd and cheer you on up there, you knucklehead."

Hundreds of people are already gathered around the foot of a makeshift stage in the distance—and some are even holding homemade E.T. signs. Oh God. This is bad. I've already messed up step one of Operation National Exposure: losing Aunt Heidi on the way.

"Nate!"

Unless Roscoe appears.

"Hiya, Foster," he says, bopping over. One thing is that grown-up men shouldn't wear big earmuffs. Ever.

"Hi, I'm Nate's aunt, Heidi." She extends a hand, and Roscoe looks like he's going to fall over. He's a bit of a lady's man, is what Asella calls him, and you've got to admit that Aunt Heidi is kind of a fox.

"Hi, I'm Nate's stage manager," he says, shaking Heidi's hand like it's a baby's rattle.

"O . . . kay," Heidi says, pulling back and gulping from her thermos. Which is totally *empty*, by the way, and already was by Queensboro Plaza twenty minutes ago. God, it's amazing to watch a real actress use a prop.

"I'll take Nate from here," Roscoe says, grabbing my shoulder. "We'll get him all suited up and then he and Jordan and I will head back to the theater. Big final dress rehearsal today!"

"Hooray," I say.

"Okay," Aunt Heidi says, grabbing my free arm and tugging me back. "But can't I stay with Nate until he goes onstage, at least?"

I know Aunt Heidi gave up a commercial audition at nine this morning, so it'll probably tick her off if she can't stay here. That being said, the audition was for some shampoo called Unforgivably Natural, and between you and me, Aunt Heidi dyes her hair every two weeks, so it would have been pretty dishonest.

Roscoe tips his fake cowboy hat at Heidi. "Can't have anyone but production staff in the actors' trailers."

He's lying. I just watched Jordan's mom scoot after him into theirs.

Aunt Heidi squats by my side, pulling my knit cap down over my ears. "You going to be okay, buddy?" she says, like I'm four and not almost fourteen. "Are you going to be *warm*?" This is the default position all ladies go to, no matter what: a child's warmth.

"Oh sure," I say, but it comes out like popcorn on a fryer, my teeth chattering like heck out here. "I'll bbbbe ttottalllly ccool."

"A little *too* cool," she says, standing up so fast that she accidentally knocks my hat off—which is hilarious, since she's become my warmth advocate. "Can we get Nate some hot tea *now*, and also get him inside his production-staff-only trailer?"

Amazing. Who needs an agent with Aunt Heidi, man killer, around?

"Well, that's all I'm trying to do, Miss," Roscoe says, this time without that huge grin. I don't think so, anyway. His moustache is so overgrown, it hides any mood change.

"Well . . . maybe Unforgivably Natural is still seeing fake-brunettes," Aunt Heidi says. "I'm going to dash. I'll see you tonight, Natey. Don't forget your steps. And don't forget to have *fun*."

No chance about the last part—I'll only have fun once I don't stomp all over Jordan's big feet—but the steps part? I've run the waltz so many times, you could cut me off at the waist and still send my legs out to perform the number.

"Love you, Aunt Heidi," I say, and she blows an air kiss and hurries off toward the subway, watching me the whole time. But I bet you *anything* she'll still sneak to the back of the crowd and watch me up there today. She's very aunty that way.

"That was close," I'm about to go, but Roscoe grabs my neck and hurries me to the curb, tucking me behind an idling cab.

"Listen, son," he says, biting at the words like

turkey jerky. "We could *both* get into hot water over all of this."

I'd love nothing more than to get into hot water right now. Heck, I'd even splurge for bubbles.

"I'm sorry!" I say. "I know I was supposed to meet you way down the street. It's just. You know *ladies*. They walk in fast-forward when it's cold out."

Roscoe tries hard not to laugh. "Lord, why do I still do this?"

I think he means show business in general, but he could mean outdoor events with children, too. Or wearing earmuffs. I would sooner lose my ears than wear muffs to school.

"I think you 'do' this," I say to Roscoe, "because you owe Asella a favor? Something about a photo in a bar."

Traffic zips past us.

"That'll be enough," he says, his eyes going wide. The cab speeds away and Roscoe points me to a trailer. Like, a *real* trailer, the kind actors hang out in on movie sets! "That's your home today. You're shar- ing it with an actress from *Call Me Stro*, since the whole world thinks you're Asella. Otherwise, they would've just set you up in Jordan's trailer."

"Sounnds ssswwell," I say, hopping up and down to stay warm. I'm probably eighty internal degrees right now, but I remind myself that in Florida—the only exotic place the Fosters have ever traveled—eighty degrees is considered a lovely day. A vacation!

"All right, let's get you *inside*," Roscoe says, pushing me along, "before *anyone* sees you."

But by the time he's saying *sees you*, I've spotted somebody we both know.

"Duck!" I whisper-scream, crouching behind Roscoe's substantial legs. "It's *Bernie the First*! At twelve o'clock!"

And there he is, walking toward us with the kind of energy that Libby's new boyfriend would use to corner me for, like, wearing earmuffs.

"Oh, he's with *us*," Roscoe says, kicking me out from behind him. "Bernie's an inside jobber."

And that's when Bernard Billings-Sapper unzips a huge plastic bag, bigger even than my strange pirate teddy bear. The one from that two-timer Genna.

"Welcome to your first TV appearance, Nathan," Bernie says. "Or, sorry: *Nate*." He holds up E.T.'s mask, a jack-o'-lantern of folds and freckles. "Congrats." He hands it to me. "You're the first person to put one of these on, little star."

And just like that, the chattering leaves my teeth and takes an express train straight for my heart. "Wow."

The Main Event For Real

(The day before previews start!)

Even in 25-degree weather, with frost dusting the treetops a powdered-sugar white, I'm piping hot, dressed head to toe as the most famous alien in the world, other than Ricky Martin.

"I'm going to hold your hand," Roscoe says, "and steer you across the promenade to the stage. So you don't run into stuff."

Here's the great thing about being the kind of kid who, even with a full range of eyesight in his everyday life, frequently runs into poles: When you've got a *mask* on, you've finally got an excuse to be a klutz. No one's gonna ask me to run around in *this* getup.

"Hi, Asella!" I hear. "Wanna run around and warm up with me?"

Ugh. It's him, Jordan Rylance, in Elliott's white T-shirt and red hoodie and brand-new costume jeans. The only giveaway that he's even playing a part is his sneakers, which are covered with plastic bags and tied at the ankle (to protect his precious feet from the snow).

"Nah, I don't need any help warming up," I'm about to say—to blow my own cover, two seconds into the mission—when Roscoe cuts in.

"Asella'll be just fine, Jordan. I think she's already pretty hot in there. Give us the thumbs-up if you're hot in there, 'Sell."

I try to give a thumbs-up and almost knock my helmet off, just because E.T.'s thumb is built like a long branch. Everyone laughs except Jordan's Mommy, who stops adjusting his microphone. "Quiet, J.J.," she says. Ninety bucks his middle name is Jesus. "Let's save that voice for America."

We're standing beneath a blazing outdoor heater, with the stage set up just beyond. It's a portable gym riser–type thing, laid out next to a beautiful stone fountain at the entrance of the park.

"I bet you've been here a million times," Jordan says, talking through his Mommy's hand—oh dear, at *me*. "On the trip where we came to New York to get my headshots taken, we shot in Central Park so I could swing from one of the lamp poles. Just like Fred Astaire in *Singin' in the Rain*."

My already sweating forehead practically splits in half. Fred *Astaire*? He means Gene Kelly, and he should be ashamed of himself, because Gene Kelly is *from* Pittsburgh. The only good thing we can even boast. Other than Clark bars. And Libby. God, I hope she's DVRing the show today.

"We booked a session with a New York photographer," Jordan's Mommy says, "because you've got to have the best if you want the best results." She takes off her leopard coat and wraps Jordan's shoulders in it. "We'd already burned through five Pittsburgh photographers, spending several thousand dollars."

"Apiece," Jordan says, real quiet, his face half-covered by the leopard hood.

"*Save* it," she says, elbowing Jordan so hard that he slips in his plastic-bag shoes. "*Save. That. Voice.* How much do we have to spend on those two little cords for you to take them seriously?"

He slurps at the tea and grits his teeth.

"And so," his mom says, "we came to Central Park and spent a small fortune." She licks her teeth free of an emergency-red lipstick that keeps migrating across her fangs. "I went without mani-pedis for a month!"

I throw my head back and shake my shoulders up and down, simulating silent film laughter. It's actually nice to know what a mani-pedi reference is, though.

"That's enough, Mother," Jordan says, gulping from his sweating thermos. "Asella doesn't need to hear all this."

"The important thing is this," she says, pulling Vaseline from her purse while simultaneously biting off a really expensive leather glove (you can tell leather is expensive if it's purple). "All the trips and all the money and all the lessons—all of them lead up to this moment. My J.J. on national TV, promoting my J.J. on Broadway."

She scoops out a margarine-size wedge of Vaseline and smoothes back Jordan's eyebrows, which are already so unruffled, they look tattooed.

Roscoe reappears, back from consulting with a pair of ladies in black sweatshirts and stocking caps. Crew people. "We should get you two back into your trailers if *Cirque: Windtasia* is going to take so long up there."

Oh! I heard about this show on a TV set in the back of a cab. (Yes, you read that right, by the way: a TV set *in the back of a cab*.) In *Windtasia*, the performers' feet never actually touch the stage. Supposed to be "spectacular in a French-Canadian sort of way," according to a reporter on New York One.

"Follow me," Roscoe says, "they can *fetch* us when they want us."

I capture a glance at this circus man hovering high above the stage by virtue of a 747-size fan below him. He really does look like the wind, if the wind wore a skintight bodysuit. "*Asella,*" Roscoe shouts. "God, I've been *saying* your *name* for *thirty* seconds."

He and I shuffle back to the girls' trailer alone, my huge feet crammed into the E.T. slippers. Which I might be outgrowing already.

"You wanna take that mask off, Nate?" Roscoe says, just as I'm struggling to the top of the third step. "And maybe get a glass of water?" I'd like nothing more, in fact, but I don't have a chance to respond. Not with Jordan suddenly bopping after us.

"Hey, Mr. Roscoe"—*Mr.* Roscoe, of all things— "could we run the number in my trailer? It's just me alone, so I don't mind if Asella's in there."

The *Cirque* performers are still garnering hoots and applause, seven of them currently airborne above the audience, like a tornado of abs.

"*Asella*, would that be all right with you?" Roscoe says.

I give a cautious thumbs-up and trudge back down the stairs, by now woozy in the suffocating costume. In fact, the stream of cool air through E.T.'s mouth vent is the only thing keeping me upright. That, and the fact that you're literally unable to sit while wearing this suit.

"Follow me," Jordan says, leading us back through the packed snow trail. But he doesn't need to point the way. His trailer is the nicest of all: a bright white mobile-home of a thing, parked just next to the stage.

"*Visitors!*" Jordan's Mommy says when we're all

inside. She's at a dressing table applying so much makeup, I wouldn't be surprised if *she* were joining the *Cirque* act. The lady is basically a bag of wind to begin with.

"Okay," Roscoe says, "you two kids wanna do a dry run of the song?" He pushes a coffee lid through his extravagant moustache.

"Kids?" Jordan's Mommy laughs. "Asella is probably *double* my age. Triple!"

This offends even me, and I'm not even the elderly in question. No chance Asella is double Mrs. Rylance's age. She's one of those moms who had a kid late in life and now pours her every ounce of soul into him. Not that I'd complain if my mom were a little more like that. The only things she ever pours into me are warnings.

"Oh, right, right," Roscoe says, chuckling. Too hard. "Didn't mean *kids*, but you know showbiz types. Kids at heart, forever." He breaks into a little tap step. There isn't a man in show business who doesn't know a little beginners' tap.

"Let's get on with the routine, then," Jordan's Mommy says, turning to us after smearing gel across her helmet of hair. She plops into a director's chair, the words *Head Mom* embroidered across the top. "Shall we have a look? I want to check Jordan's angles."

"Well, that's actually *Monica's* job," Roscoe says,

eyes flicking to his cell phone. "I don't know why Monica's not here yet, but angle checking is what the dance team handles."

"Does Monica live in New Jersey, by any chance?" says Jordan's Mommy.

Jordan looks like he's about to fall asleep on his feet—swaying ever so slightly, like a FOR SALE sign in the breeze. Every house back home is for sale except ours, because "nobody's gonna buy this piece of junk even if we had somewhere else to move," according to the Dad of the Year.

"She *does*, actually," Roscoe says. "Monica lives in Jersey City." He's frowning at Mrs. Rylance now—at least that's the position of his moustache.

"*Lincoln Tunnel suspicious package* is trending on Twitter," Mrs. Rylance says, holding up her own iPhone. "This *Monica* gal won't be here for hours. Snap to it, Jordan. Top of the song."

Whoa. Mrs. Rylance claps her knees, leans forward, and proceeds to mouth Jordan's lyrics along with him. It's twenty seconds into the routine before I remember I'm even *in* the routine.

"Look alive, Asella," Mrs. Rylance bellows through a smile that could cut cheese or maybe even steel. "You're on camera in fifteen minutes."

"How do you *know* all of this?" Roscoe says, checking his walkie-talkie for signal strength.

"I slipped the head camera man a twenty when we got here," Mrs. Rylance says, "and he keeps texting me updates on the shooting schedule." Her phone vibrates.

"He *what*?" Roscoe says.

Mrs. Rylance plays with an earring. "Learn the system or die," she says to Jordan, who nods so hard, his T-shirt comes untucked.

"Back to the top then, Mommy?" Jordan says, yawning.

"*Yes*, back to the top, for continuity. And if I catch you yawning one more time, darling"—with every word, her mouth grows bigger and smilier, like if Ronald McDonald went on a murder spree—"my Manolo Blahniks are going to end up down your throat, yes?"

She lifts a leg and wags a foot at Jordan, who stifles another yawn.

"Five," she says, and Jordan goes, "six, seven, eight" and starts to sing again.

"*Left in a place where I've nothing to hide, left with a dream that is pent up inside, I'm all alone but I've also got you. You, you, new and true.*"

He turns to me.

He looks really hard into E.T.'s mouth.

"Okay, stop, stop," Mrs. Rylance says, hopping up on her Blahniks. "Did we say we were going to hit the word *new* or the word *true*, J.J.-baby."

"*New,*" he mutters.

"I can't *hear* you," she says.

But moments ago, he wasn't even *allowed* to talk. Moments ago he wasn't permitted to even flap his little gold vocal cords in the wind.

"*New,*" he says now, louder. "We're emphasizing *new,* because anything new is more important than anything that's true." He speaks like a child robot, like the kind of kid who actually—and this makes me shudder, even in this mega-hot costume—studies for tests.

"That's right, J.J.," Mrs. Rylance says, but she's not talking to J.J. She's talking to me. "*Ladies* know that anything new is better than anything that's true." She jangles a gold watch at me, and I realize I'm supposed to react like a lady, so I cover my crotch for some reason. Idiot. "This might not be *true* gold—hello, Canal Street knock-offs!—but it's brand-hot-*new!*"

"You got it, Mom," Jordan says. "So we should go back to the top. For continuity."

"Actually," Roscoe says, "I think what we should *do* is throw a robe over Jordan's costume and then get him a little tea, or chocolate. Or something. He looks exhausted." No doubt he was up all night rehearsing. "Gotta pep him up." Roscoe fiddles with the knob on his walkie-talkie. "And, to be honest, Mrs. Rylance, I don't love the dynamic here. You are *really* not supposed to be coaching the kid on lyrics."

Mrs. Rylance erupts into a shocking cackle that rattles the whole trailer. "Who do you think would coach him if I didn't? *Dewey*? Mr. Dewey Decimal System?"

I search for the library joke in there but decide there isn't one—though I do feel pretty checked out.

"Mommy, stop," Jordan says, his eyes suddenly wet. "Just stop."

"All I'm saying is, if you're going to slap *my* kid's name on a marquee, expect me to come on strong and fight for his performance."

"We've got plenty of kids fighting for his performance," Roscoe says. I turn to him. What did he mean by that? "Plenty of *people*, I mean. Plenty of people are looking out for him."

"I think I know what you meant, and I don't like it." Mrs. Rylance leaps up from the director's chair. "You bet your patootie there are other boys fighting for his limelight."

"*Mother.*"

"Jordan Rylance?" A muffled voice creeps through the trailer door, followed by a couple of knocks. "Mr. Rylance, you're onstage in ten minutes."

Jordan's face goes from sleepy to white, panic mode switched on.

"That's right, baby boy," his Mommy says, "let's see that adrenaline pump."

"Listen," Roscoe says, "I'm going to go get Asella some juice, or something. You coming along, 'Sell?"

I jump at the chance to get away, but Mrs. Rylance is barreling past us before I so much as pivot.

"Where are *you* going?" Roscoe says.

"The camera man just texted." She's fishing a wallet from a leopard pocket. "I'm going to speak with him."

For a moment, it's just Roscoe, me, Jordan, and a swirl of snow blowing through the door frame. I lift an E.T. slipper to follow Roscoe back to our trailer, dying for a moment to breathe, when Jordan grabs my arm. Even through my rubber sleeve, he's got a pretty incredible grip for such a puny kid.

"Please don't go," he says. His royal blue eyes are staring up at E.T.'s, the poor moron. My real eyes are easily two feet below. "I *have* to go over the dance break at least once. If this doesn't go well . . . if this doesn't go *perfectly*, she'll kill me."

Roscoe hesitates by the door. "*Asella?* Thumbs-up you stay with Jordan and rehearse, thumbs-down you come with me for juice. Or whatever a girl likes at this hour."

But I don't even debate.

"Okay then," Roscoe says. "Thumbs-up." He looks out into the cold. "Listen, you two: You're onstage in a jiff. I'm running to Asella's trailer to get the finger-wand hookup from Bernie."

The wand! We never plugged in the finger wand, for the final moment in the number when Jordan and Mackey touch fingers. Asella says E.T.'s is supposed to turn red, and that I have to *activate* it by pressing some internal button in the costume. But I've never rehearsed with it. It's all a theory.

"I'll be back in five minutes," Roscoe says. "Be ready to go then." He starts to leave but turns right around. "And, you know what, you two? Have a blast. This is *exciting.*" He rolls his eyes in the direction of Jordan's mom, ten feet away from the trailer and brokering some deal. You can tell because she's grabbed a guy's clipboard. "But it isn't brain surgery," Roscoe calls back.

The door shuts, and it's just us.

"Easy for him to say," Jordan goes, shaking his head. "He doesn't have a mom with five credit cards. And a dad with zero jobs." He laughs at his own joke, but it's a sad laugh, like a butterfly without wings or a fire without heat. "I shouldn't have said that. Please don't tell the others. Especially not the kids."

"Your dad doesn't have a job?" I want to say.

For once, I want to rip my head off and *talk* to the kid. To tell him I had no idea. That it doesn't make sense that a family that seems so rich, with Manolo Blankets and private voice lessons and wristwatches the color of an Oscar, could have a jobless dad.

But there's no time for that.

"Let's go right to the dance break," Jordan says. "I could do these lyrics backward in my sleep. Literally. I had to, before I was allowed to sleep."

I turn to face the trailer's mirrored wall (always use available mirrors, according to Libby) and gear up for my big moment. After Elliott tells E.T. he could never imagine having a better friend, they're supposed to do this sort of weird male-waltz thing.

"Good," Jordan says, halfway through, when I'm circling him so fast my mask clamps start to rattle. "You've gotten superquick at this part!"

We're building toward the final position, with our fingers touching, and Jordan launches into the last lyric: *"Meeting you meant I finally got to be me."*

And then we're done.

We both stop, our shoulders heaving, and a faint trail of perspiration glimmers on Jordan's upper lip. I bet his mom sends him to bed without tofu if she so much as *catches* him sweating.

"Okay, good," he says. He's still both zonked and freaked, though, his eyes checking the corners of the room, as if his Mommy hooked up hidden cameras to capture his every missed step. "I guess we'll just wait for Roscoe's wand-finger thing. Maybe we should . . . sit."

But he doesn't move. His eyes drop from E.T.'s and settle on my mesh hole, looking straight through and starting to squint. At my real eyes. "You okay in there? You haven't made a peep." He leans in. "I'm so nervous I could throw up."

He turns and looks into the mirror. *Meeting you meant I finally got to be me.* He looked so honest on that. So unforced. And in one clear moment, I . . . get it. I get why he got Elliott, and I didn't.

Jordan's more talented than I am.

"Are you *sniffling*?" Jordan says.

Thumbs-down.

He laughs. "It sounded like you were sniffling. But your voice was really low."

I shrug, the rubber suit squeaking. Jordan yawns again.

"Maybe I'll have a little coffee," Jordan says. "My mom would *murder* me if she knew I've been drinking it with Genna on breaks. But it's so *good*. It's really mature."

"We're not allowed to eat or drink in costume, Jordan," I wish I could say. I really do.

He starts to lift a huge carafe that's sitting out for the adults. But just then, his determination is broken by the crowd's alarmingly loud whistles and cheers. *Cirque* is done.

So is Jordan.

He is covered—no, *drenched*—in spilled coffee.

"Oh *God,* no!" he screams, staring at his formerly

bright-white T-shirt in the mirror. "Oh God. Oh God. She'll kill me. She'll *murder* me. They'll fire me and-and-and we won't be able to pay for our house. Or the swimming pool. Or the koi pond."

"It's not so bad," I want to lie.

He poured an entire steaming carafe of java down his own shirt, two minutes before we're going live. His collar looks like a coffee filter.

"Oh no, if I cry . . . if I cry, my makeup will run." He tilts his head back, just like the nurse taught me do to when the bullies got to my nose. "I can't wear this T-shirt on the air. Elliott doesn't drink coffee. Oh God, Asella."

It's not just his Mommy who'll kill him. If he doesn't nail it today, the producers will have his neck. *E.T.* is already a big question mark on Broadway— an industry joke, according to Asella. This could turn that question mark into, like, a period.

"What am I going to do?" he wails.

And that's when I do it.

"I've got a white T-shirt on," I say, unlatching the E.T. helmet and tossing it onto the dressing table. "You have to unzip the back of the suit, and then I can give you my shirt."

He watches me through the mirror, his face frozen. At the very least, I've stopped him from crying. In fact: Is he . . . grinning a little bit? "This is impossible."

"No, it's not." I give the thumbs-up. "It's me. Your old friend Nate."

"I can't . . . *what* are you doing here?" He turns to look at me in living color. "We cannot let my mom . . . does *Roscoe* know?"

"Roscoe's in on it, Jordan. Everyone is." Not everyone, but for the purposes of drama, yes. "Learn the system or die." I flip around so he can get to my zipper.

"I can't wear your T-shirt, you *monkey*," he says. You can tell his family says *monkey* as a swearword.

"Or what? You're going to let your Mommy see you in a coffee-stained costume?"

That does it. He whips back to the mirror and screams.

"Jordan Rylance"—from the trailer door, some girl's voice booms—"we need you onstage in sixty *seconds*."

"I've got the finger hookup!" Roscoe bounds up the stairs, shaking the trailer so hard that Jordan loses his balance and crashes into the makeup table. That said, he'd already gotten pretty wobbly on his feet in the last thirty seconds.

"Oh God," Roscoe says.

"Oh *monkey*!" Mrs. Rylance screams, entering right after. "What's going on? *Why* is this mongrel here?" She takes in Jordan's new state. *"And what happened to your shirt?!"*

"Mommy, I-I-I," he starts, his face going white to purple to red, like that bubble gum that changes berry flavors. But there's nothing sweet here.

"It was my fault," I say, managing to unzip my own costume, cracking my back while I'm at it. I'm really growing up these days. "It was totally my fault. I was drinking coffee. And tripped. And Jordan should take my T-shirt."

"We need a boy and a woman onstage!" A girl in a headset and black sweats stampedes into the trailer. "You're not a woman," she says, tilting her head at me.

"He's not an anything," Mrs. Rylance says. "He's an *understudy*."

"Mom."

"Enough!" Roscoe shouts. He points at me: "Shirt off, now." He points at Jordan: "Shirt off, now."

I've never done this, changing in front of another boy. Back home, it's either skip gym altogether and fake a migraine (WebMD is remarkable for how specific they get with symptoms) or go into the bathroom stall to change my shirt. I'd never do this under *any* circumstance.

"Twenty seconds," a production assistant calls through Roscoe's walkie-talkie, "or we're sending *Cirque* back out."

But this isn't just any circumstance.

"No!" Roscoe shouts. "We are not getting pre-empted by theatrical *wind*."

Jordan and I switch shirts, and I turn my back on him as fast as I possibly can, likely leaving a little belly in my wake.

"Wow, this thing is so *sweaty*," he calls out. But he doesn't even sound ticked off, somehow. Like, at all.

"Oh, don't you worry, J.J.," his mom says. "We'll have Daddy draw up some *papers* on this kid."

"No, we won't," Jordan says, tucking my T-shirt into his jeans. Roscoe fiddles with Jordan's microphone, and I zip myself back into E.T.'s costume, my shoulders straining in the reach. "We aren't suing anyone, Mom. Not this time. Not Nate." Jordan stares at me. "Just drop it. He knows."

"Knows *what*?" she shrieks.

"*Run* for the stage," the crew lady shouts. "*Now.*"

"Nate knows we're bankrupt," Jordan yells, pulling free from Roscoe's grip. "And I don't care that he does."

"The plastic bags!" Roscoe says, pointing at Jordan's feet. "Take them off!"

"*There isn't time!*" The crew woman grabs Jordan by the waist and tosses him up onto the stage. He lands the way a kitten might fall from an end table, in one perfectly quiet poof. One perfectly adorable quiet poof.

The crowd roars its approval and Jordan turns to face them, bolted to the stage with plastic feet, the opening chords of music ringing out from a speaker mounted in the trees.

We all pile out the doorway of his trailer and stare up at him.

"My God," I think we all say together.

I'd die in this situation. If I were him, I'd lose my voice or pee my pants. I'd panic or cry, singing too fast or not singing at all.

"Left in a place where I've nothing to hide," he starts to sing, his voice even, perfect, *"left with a dream that is pent up inside . . ."*

Maybe the biggest surprise of my year isn't that I'm on Broadway. Maybe it's that some other kid, from the good part of town—outside of Jankburg's dreary county lines, marked by a sad broken fence that nobody's bothered to paint—might have something in common with me. At least in the family finance department.

"I'm all alone but I've also got you."

The surprise of my century is that Jordan really was born to be a star. And I was born to be an understudy. And maybe the biggest surprise is that I'm starting to be cool with that.

"You're supposed to be onstage, Nate," Roscoe says, really quiet.

"Yeah," I say through the mesh. "But let's give Jordan the first verse. I'll enter on the dance break."

"He's amazing," Jordan's mom says. But like a real one. A real mom who's proud, wearing things she probably can't pay for. She's got jewels like Mom's got orchids. But at least Mrs. Rylance is here.

"Yes, he is," I say, relatching the E.T. mask and heading for the stage. "He's amazing."

But This Was Supposed to Be the Best Day Ever

(The. Morning. Of. The. Show.)

I didn't think anyone would see the photo.

The excuse that I truly believe—the excuse I will take to my grave, which could come any day, because skin cancer runs in my family—is that Jordan did such a magnificent job up there yesterday, that I momentarily misplaced my common sense. And so, when I yanked my E.T. mask off after the number ended, and took a self-portrait in the trailer mirror (Mrs. Rylance wouldn't take it for me), and sent the photo to Libby—

"I never would have thought she'd post it on Facebook," I say. "I really didn't! The crowd, the thin Central Park air . . . they did a trick on my brain, Dewey."

Apparently there's a company policy about not taking any pictures of E.T. with his head off. Something about not "giving away the magic." Who knew?

"I don't want to *hear* it—" Dewey says, pausing just after.

"Nate," Calvin whispers into his ear.

"Nate," Dewey says, louder than he needs to. We're in stage management's cold basement office, the cement bricks catching voices like a glove. Roscoe sulks in the corner of his own hangout.

"Please don't scroll through my photos," I say to Dewey, who's poking at my Nokia like it's a prehistoric relic. Even though it can't do e-mail or Facebook or anything, it actually takes pretty nifty photos, if you're good at squinting.

"You've given up any privacy rights by doing something so stupid, Nate," Roscoe says, grabbing my phone and tossing it into his drawer. "Any rights at all."

"Guys," Calvin says, always the voice of reason, "aren't we being a little harsh here?"

"No," Dewey says, snapping. "*Everything* has led up to this moment. And this kid is Facebooking photos of himself as E.T. At an event he wasn't even supposed to *be* at?"

Roscoe buries his face in his hands.

"Where's the backstage wizardry there, huh?" Dewey says. "This kid's making me look like a total idiot. This was my *moment*, Cal." Dewey stands to look out the window. This is difficult, because we're in a basement.

"It's still your moment, Dew," Calvin says.

I raise my hand.

"Yes?" Calvin says, his face a painful cramp, like he wants to be helping me but I'm making it . . . difficult. I remember this as the expression Anthony had the first time I got on our school bus wearing turquoise. And I don't mean the color.

"I just wanted to say again that I didn't upload the photo. I texted it to my best friend, whose mother is struggling with health issues, and my friend posted it on Facebook. To help promote us."

The three guys burst into a merry laughter that is edged with knives.

"Unless your best friend is Riedel at the *Post*, we have a strict policy about *not* Tweeting or Facebooking sensitive backstage information." I'm not even sure which one of these men is talking now. "There was an entire company meeting about this."

"Yes," I say, raising my hand again, "but that meeting was held, I've only now learned, on one of the days I was in cardio-aerobics with Monica. So I can't really be blamed for not knowing." Or can I? I don't know much about New York laws. "Can I be arrested for this?"

They've got nothing, and Calvin looks to the other guys with a Well? sort of shrug, but that doesn't stop Roscoe.

"*I* think," he says, "I need to apologize to the company for bungling the event, myself—and obviously we're going to need to sidebar with Asella, too—and then we'll have to come up with some sort of reprimand for our Nate."

I think he's kind of teasing, but then Dewey cuts in with, "Absolutely. Nathan Flosser should . . . should sit out of rehearsal today."

"Foster," Calvin and I both go, but Dewey waves us off.

"Normally I'd agree, Dewey," Roscoe says, "but we can't afford to be down a cast member. First preview and everything. Gotta have all men on deck."

The room gets superstill and superawkward. Still, it's nice to be called a man. "I didn't think it would go viral," I offer. "I really didn't."

It's true. Apparently not a single production photo had been released to the press before now, with hopes the public's curiosity would lead to boffo box office (Asella's phrase—and why *isn't* Asella here?). And so this first-glimpse peek at my pimply grin popping out of the E.T. collar? It went viral. Libby's photo was so reposted and shared, a news place in Pittsburgh picked up on it yesterday, and then this thing called the AP caught on, and then it went international.

And then Aunt Heidi sent me to bed with a couple of Children's Tylenol last night because I was crying so hard. She offers me Children's Tylenol for basically everything, like even when I don't want to brush my teeth.

"You can't count on anything going viral or *not* going viral," Dewey says, this time to himself. "If you could, my first four video games would have been hits."

Roscoe lifts the theater's intercom microphone and announces, "Actors, welcome home." He always calls the theater *home*. You'd think that'd be amazing and comforting, but these days it reminds me of my real home, where I'm also not so welcome. "We're doing notes in the house with Dewey. After a short announcement. So . . . happy first preview!"

"Where are you going?" Dewey says, just as I'm picking up my bookbag.

"To . . . um . . . to my dressing room to get my notebook?"

I'm the only kid with a paper notebook. Everyone else types their notes into their phones, but (a) my Nokia would internally burn if I tried that, and (b) I think it's rude. I don't even like pencils, but I'll use one for notes from a director because I saw Asella doing that and it just seems *right*.

"Fine," Dewey says. "You can take notes, but then lay low the rest of the day."

"Okay."

"I really don't want to see you in my sights."

"He heard you, Dewey," Calvin says.

"And I'm *disturbed*, by the way," Dewey says, "by you carrying that *ketchup* bottle around."

"Sorry," I say. "It wasn't my idea." He's right, though. A ketchup bottle is tucked beneath my arm. Long story.

"Nothing seems to be," Dewey says. "I keep waiting for you to *have* an idea, but you're so busy running into other actors that we should have taken an insurance policy out on you."

He's talking about me almost breaking Genna's leg (she's *fine*) and also a time when I stepped directly onto Mackey's head. This image, God knows why, propels me to say: "At least Mackey didn't have to stand outside in the cold yesterday, right?"

Roscoe gives me a stern warning glance, the kind my dad gives me whenever I practice pirouettes near his signed Roberto Clemente baseball. It's too late, though. Dewey sinks onto the piano bench and practically starts crying. "Stop. Talking. About. The. Event."

So much for the deal we made yesterday—the Rylances and Roscoe and me. We agreed to keep the whole thing a secret: As long as I'd never tell anyone that the Rylances are up to their glass E.T. eyeballs in debt, they'd never tell anyone I subbed in for Asella.

Whoops!

"It was a *gift*," I say, thrusting the ketchup bottle in the air and nearly squeezing a dollop onto Dewey's shirt. "By the way."

"Nice gift," he says, snorting and getting meaner. He was probably a math geek in school. Math geeks are the most insecure geeks of all, so they can be the quietest and deadliest kind of bully.

"I know it's weird," I say, looking at my Heinz bottle, which I really *have* been lugging around since I was called into stage management's office this morning. "But when your secret admirer leaves you ketchup, and a note saying, '*My cheeks go as red as tomatoes around you,*' what are you gonna do? Toss it?"

This stops them dead. I didn't mean it to. I thought I'd gain favor by hinting about my sort-of girlfriend. Most guys are more comfortable around other guys who've got girls on their tails. (Even if the girl on your tail is also after Jordan's tail and maybe every boy's tail.)

"Red as tomatoes," Dewey goes, but then he trails off, grabbing his iced green tea (he's the kind of guy who drinks iced green tea, which I think says a lot about his level of sanity to begin with, right?) and jetting out of the room.

And it's only when Dewey is six seconds out the door that I realize stage management's phone is jingling itself off the hook. And it's *another* three seconds before

I register Roscoe saying, *"Dear God, are you serious?"*

And finally, half a minute after Dewey bolted from my inquisition, Roscoe grabs the door frame and swings his head into the hallway.

"Dewey," he hollers, almost like he's calling a guy in for grits on a farm (I saw half of *Gone with the Wind* in fourth grade).

Roscoe shakes his head and says a ton of swear-words—really bad ones, like Biblically bad—and grabs the intercom again: "Dewey, to stage management's office please. Now. *Now*, now."

Very specific.

"What's up, Rosc?" Calvin says, staring at the receiver in Roscoe's hand. I wedge myself behind a garbage can.

"Houston, we've got a problem," Roscoe says, opening up a big binder on his desk after making a Texas reference that's probably only appropriate for grown-ups?

"What's the latest, what's the latest," Dewey says, back in the basement in a video game dash. "Did the kid Tweet a photo of me *yelling* at him or something?"

"Worse," Roscoe says, shoving me out the door, cowboy-booting it shut in my dust.

What did I do *now*? Were they offended about my girlfriend reference? Do they know it's a total . . . embellishment?

"Gulp," I actually say, after whispering a series of flops that probably gets the ghosts of our theater pretty riled up. A mouse runs along the hallway floorboard, and I'd jump away if there were anything to jump up on. So instead I squeal like a kettle. And it's just after my vocal cords have stopped doing the tango that I hear Roscoe, muffled but true, shouting his head off in the stage manager's office.

"You don't have a star for the performance tonight, Dewey. We need to call in Nora Von Escrow and the rest of the producers."

"What the" (extraordinarily bad word) *"are you talking about?"* Dewey says.

"We're going to have to cancel the first preview."

And that's when Dewey screams so murderously loud, the mouse and I look at each other and run in opposite directions, him into a hole and me directly into Asella—who's got her script, a bag of lozenges, and the smoke of fire in two saucer-wide eyes.

"We," she says, "have to talk."

Is Somebody *Dead*?

(The. Day. Of. The Show.)

With the cast called into the auditorium for an emergency company meeting, you'll get why I'm surprised that Asella has me way in the *back* of the house, where first-time patrons will be filtering through in just a couple hours. Or not.

"What's going *on*, Asella?" I say. Really, I grunt it, because she's got me doing sit-ups. Is she punishing me for getting her in trouble because of the event? *Is* she in trouble? "Are you mad at me?" Did she lose custody of Doc in small-person-claims court?

But she places one shoe one inch above my one and only face. "*Quiet.*" She taps my nose with a Ked. "I'm asking the questions here." Oh God.

The lights in the house flicker twice, signaling the beginning of a rehearsal. And you'd think, given the mounting drama around here, that all my castmates would be buzzing—like, at the level of honey making. But they're not making a peep. They're gathered near the orchestra pit, quiet as a funeral—though I *can* make out Genna, yammering on about how her mom wouldn't let her get her ears pierced until she was five. The girl is oblivious.

"Okay," I say, finishing my set of three sit-ups and taking a thirty-second cooldown. "If this is about my idiotic self-portrait on Facebook, and getting us caught, I can expl—"

"Ladies and gentlemen." Roscoe's voice is unsteady for the first time, and I leap to my feet to join Asella, who's suddenly peering over the back-row railing. "Any stragglers, let's all move to the front of the house. Nora will be here in a moment and I want to make sure everyone can hear her."

The funeral comes alive. The very mention of our producer's name sends the cast into, like, *Ben Hur: The Sequel* screams.

"Let's talk later," I say, heading to join the company when Asella (literally) grips me by the shirt.

"Remember the last time we were at the Koreaaaah Spaaaaaah?"

"When I finally allowed them to put clear nail polish on me?"

"Exactly," she says. "But this isn't about that."

"What are we all doing here?" a voice from the audience cries out. "I have to get back to a client in MiMa by noon."

"That's Genna's *dad*," Asella whispers, sighing so hard I can smell tuna fish and fear on her breath. "They've called in *all* the parents to this meeting."

Well, this can't be good at all. This can't be anything even orbiting Planet Good.

"Yoo-hoo!" Nora Von Escrow, British producer to end all, strides into the house. You can tell it's her, even from back here, because the teenagers and dancers are clapping. Entrance applause is only reserved for TV stars and the British, according to Libby.

"Why are we *hiding* back here, Asella?" I say. And that's when Roscoe catches sight of us, because that's when my voice gets really loud.

"Jiminy *Christmas*, Nate," he calls out. "Get down *front*. We're having a *meeting*."

He can't even see Asella, who'll probably sneak underneath all the seats and arrive just in time for the bagels that Nora always brings when she visits the cast.

"One second, sir!" Asella yells from a crouch, doing a remarkable impersonation of my voice. Frankly it's transfixing. "Answer me one thing," she says to me, now, her eyes the dots of two question marks. *"How confident are you?"*

I watch Roscoe thump his way up the aisle.

"In your ability to play E.T.?" I ask Asella.

It's a remarkable amount of trust she's putting in

me. Until only recently, I didn't know a legitimate actor from a mailman. In fact, I can remember only two summers ago, when Libby would grill me on where I was, "just before a scene." I'd go, "What do you mean, *where*? I was looking through your old Playbills, wishing I was Stephanie Mills." And Libby would go, "*No*, Nate, in the actual SCENE. Where were you in the SCENE prior to this SCENE, because acting is MAKE-BELIEVE."

Libby's the kind of girl who talks in all caps.

And my point, folks, is that I can hardly MAKE-BELIEVE that Asella's asking for my opinion on her performance. I can hardly believe it either.

"You're better than Mackey at the part, Asella," I say, taking her hand.

And just as she un-bites her lip and draws a breath to confess something monumental—she's squinting the way grown-ups always do when they have to tell you your guinea pig was killed in a dryer accident—I am ripped from her sweaty-palmed grip.

"*We* are," Roscoe says, "*waiting.*"

He barrels me down the aisle, and I see Nora standing over everyone in front of the orchestra pit, with a glossy fur coat looped to the top of her throat.

"*Sit*," she says to me. Roscoe plops me into an aisle seat near the front, my least favorite place in any classroom. "Listen up now, everyone." Nora looks like an alien herself, because her hair's in a million foil folds. Just like Mom's when her friend Pat comes over and does Mom's hair in our basement.

"*So,*" Nora and Roscoe and Dewey and Garret Charles all say, as if rehearsed. This ignites a light titter among the actor-folk.

"So *what*?" Keith's mom calls out. Each child has a parent sitting next to him or her. Except yours untruly.

"Here's the thing," Dewey starts. "The very thing."

But Garret is having none of this preamble, rising, taking off his first-preview overcoat and sailing it across the orchestra pit, where it lands onstage in front of the ghost light. Further murmuring ensues.

"Let's all come to attention, people," he says, rapping a cane against the floor. "We've just had an emergency production meeting outside in Nora's Town Car."

"Yes," she says, as if to confirm.

Asella snorts. She's just behind me, standing in the aisle with hip-glued hands.

"There is troubling news," Garret says.

Oh God, we're closing.

"There's *quite* troubling news."

We're closing before we're opening.

They've pulled the rights. My photo leak has caused too many people to phone in and cancel their tickets.

"Occasionally," Garret continues, taking a glass of tea from Monica, "an occurrence befalls a company just before the first preview."

"An *incident*," Nora says, suddenly tugging foil from her hair, then rolling it into small balls and tucking the result into her fur pockets. The lady is so skinny, I wouldn't be surprised if she *snacked* on these treasures. The iron content alone has got to be pretty high.

"Is somebody *dead*?" Genna's dad says, and this sets the children off. Everyone but me.

I'm certain they're about to call me out, and at that point I may as *well* be dead. The *Pittsburgh Post-Gazette* will finally do an article about me: "Local Boy Makes Bad, Closes *E.T.*, Comes Home to Town Square Hanging; Older Brother Thrilled." The headline wouldn't be that long probably but you get what I mean.

"Nobody's dead!" Dewey shouts, his eyes tennis-matching back and forth between Nora and Garret, who bookend him like British umpires. "Nobody's even a *little* dead!"

At this point, Calvin actually walks down the aisle and manually seats Dewey, who is shaking so hard, his entire hairstyle has shifted before our very eyes.

"Is the show closing?" a mother shouts.

"Okay, let's be *clear*, gang." My hero, Calvin, takes

control—and nobody stops him. *"Jordan Rylance has lost his voice."*

What?

"Jordan Rylance stood in the cold yesterday, and sang his guts out, and he seems to have completely lost the ability to sing."

"Let me cut to the curry," Garret Charles says, probably pulling British vaudeville phrases out of his trunk of a skull. "We don't have an Elliott."

"What about the understudies?" somebody shouts.

"What about my boy?" Keith's mom calls out. She's already holding a bunch of flowers and balloons, and this makes me miss my mom's floral shop. The low stakes of life back home. "Keith's the Elliott understudy!"

"So's my son!" another mom says.

But both their sons, nice enough boys if you can get past how appalling most boys are, whisper under their breaths at exactly the same time: "Shut *up*, Mom."

See? The thing is: None of the understudies are ready. How could they be? We barely know our own parts, most of us. There's never been a formal understudy rehearsal. It's every actor for himself around here, like if the *Titanic* were a musical, which it was, and which illustrates my point if you knew how quickly it closed.

"Your *sons*, yes." Garret Charles showcases a deadly grin. "The complicated detail about rehearsing any new show, mothers, is that—on paper or not—no understudy is ever *ready* to go on."

Calvin cuts in—"barely by the second week into official performances, let alone previews." His whole job is to get understudies up to speed *after* we open. Calvin appears to have wet his pants, unless his jeans are polka-dotted. "So we're up the creek without a paddle."

"We're up the *ocean* without a life vest," Nora says. Her face loses color and even muscle definition.

But I'm barely taking her in, because I'm hunting for Jordan in our crowd. Weird, right?

We learned in Health class that when people lose a relative, it takes a while to fully believe it. It's really difficult to grip the whole thing at once. And so my eyes search the theater, convinced this is a sick sort of joke. And it's only when I realize that Jordan's mother isn't here either that the storm cloud of it all settles directly above my own head.

"Thus," Garret says, "we've made the very difficult decision—"

He suddenly turns to Dewey, of all people, to complete the sentiment. But Dewey is burrowed so deeply into his seat, he's beginning to turn the color of the cushion.

"—we've made the very difficult decision to cancel the first preview."

Panic.

Children scurry to parents' arms, stars dial their agents, and a grandparent in a wheelchair somehow stands, wagging his *Reader's Digest* in the air. "But this will spell disaster in the news!"

"Yes," Nora says, swallowing hard and for the first time not looking theatrically dramatic but instead like the real thing. "This is precisely what we worry about too. Nobody enjoys the taste of blood like the press—"

When she says this, I swear her fur coat actually laughs a bit.

"—but this is the fate we've been dealt."

"This is *exactly* what the media has wanted all along," Dewey says, hopping to his feet, and looking furious and shell-shocked at once. "The story they've been crafting for weeks. Months! That I couldn't *back* it. That a video-game director couldn't, quote, *helm* a Broadway *show*. Who says 'helm' anymore, anyway!"

"Pull it *together*, man," Garret says.

But he doesn't. "They're going to be Tweeting a storm!" He doesn't pull it together in the least.

"If we're lucky," Garret says, laying a sad old hand on Dewey's rumpled shoulder. "If we're blessed, the *worst* they'll do is Tweeter."

This should cause misplaced giggles, but it doesn't. Not at all.

"But as we know—" Monica decides to join the squad, her voice as sharp as peanut brittle and not nearly as comforting "—there are plenty of shows that got past canceled first previews and went on to become huge hits."

But that's not true. The sequel to *Phantom*, called *Love Never Dies*, *did* die. A ferocious public death. They canceled their first preview and never recovered. This is a terrible omen, like waking up after losing a tooth only to find you *owe* your parents money.

"And so here is what's what!" Garret says, elbowing Monica out of the way, and spilling tea all over what appears to be four separate cashmere scarves, strangling his neck in agreement. "We will cancel the next three days of shows and use the time to prep Jordan's understudies."

"And if he isn't healthy by then," Nora says, but she doesn't have a backup plan. Or else her tongue is playing Hide-and-Seek.

Dewey has had enough, and he runs to an exit door and races through it. And when we all turn to watch him flee, out onto a cold winter street on the afternoon of our first canceled preview, I expect him to barrel into theatergoers, snaked around the block. Early fans. Gawkers.

But he doesn't. We watch as Dewey slams into dozens of cameramen, snapping away. They've heard. Word has leaked. We're going to cancel our first previews, announcing to a city that's already got their knives out that we are, like, indeed worth stabbing.

"As I was saying . . ." Garret begins. But even he, an aged rock of steadiness, loses his footing.

Our child star is sick. Likely because I made him wear my sweaty T-shirt in twenty-degree weather—which propels me into the type of shuddering that probably means we caught the same flu.

Nora races to the exit and returns moments later with Dewey, tumbling in after her.

"My God!" Asella shouts.

Dewey's sweater is torn! He's been mobbed!

"Don't anyone go out there," he says, thrashing, pulling away from Nora. "Don't anyone talk to the press."

"What did they ask!" calls an alto.

"What did they want?" screams a tenor.

"They want to know if we've got a show."

A sad voice tinkles like a broken bell: "And what did you tell them?" It's Genna, who must be devastated about Jordan. Her Jordan.

"I just shrugged," Dewey says, performing a sad little act like in one of those terrible cop-show reenactments. "And I said, 'You'll have to talk to the producer.'"

Nora takes her purse and whacks Dewey across the

shoulders, and the grandfather in the wheelchair takes his kid and shields her eyes. "This is a circus!" he yells.

"Hear hear," a mother shouts.

And just as the room falls into the sort of anarchy usually reserved for the *Miss Saigon* evacuation scene, Asella taps me on the shoulder. "Hoist me up," she says.

"What?" I call out above the din.

"Just hold my *legs* steady—" she hikes herself up to stand on the armrest of my chair "—so I don't careen to my death."

I do as told, ever her dutiful golden retriever.

"We are not canceling the first preview!"

The temperature in the theater drops by a full degree, reacting to the only voice in the whole company that's naturally amplified enough to draw the room's attention.

"What was that?" Garret says, shushing the noisiest of my kid-mates. "What was that again, Asella?"

"We," she says, pausing until the room is as reverent as a church at eleven, "are *not* canceling the first preview."

"What in Midtown Heaven are you *talking* about," says Nora, picking sparkles out of Dewey's hair. (Her purse is beaded—or *was*, before the assault against him basically blew it to smithereens.)

"The first preview of *E.T.: The Musical*," Asella

says, "will commence this evening at eight on the clock."

For a moment I forget that I'm Asella's primary source of balance, and when my grip goes slack and she tumbles into my lap, I instinctively swing her directly upright again, like she's my dummy. She is now hovering *above* the armrest.

"Exactly *what* are you imagining?" Nora calls. "We don't have a *star*."

"Nate Foster is going on tonight."

What what is what what tonight?

I swear the basement mouse is the only thing you can hear, stirring mischief behind the walls of the theater. The building falls so quiet that you can practically hear the water heating in the boiler.

"You've lost your mind, old girl," Dewey says to Asella, his voice softer, even, than Nora's slack jowls. (She's very jowly, which you only notice when she's staring *right* at you.)

"I've worked with him behind the scenes for over a month," Asella says, her voice gaining authority. "He's got the part down cold." Garret grunts but refuses to look away. "And Nate's been *cut* from so many numbers, all the kid's had to do, throughout all of tech, is sit in the audience. Tracking Jordan throughout."

Staring at him, she doesn't even have to say.

"He can do it."

And here, I give Monica the dance assistant credit: She stands, folds her arms, pinches her expression, wiggles her head a little, and makes a Well, I've heard of *worse* ideas kind of face at Dewey. But he withers her with his stare.

"This is ludicrous," Nora says. "Am I to trust *one* person who's seen him do this?"

"*Two.*"

My Aunt in shining armor.

"Two people. Nate can do it."

She must have gotten the message from stage management and rushed here after the real parents.

"I've watched him play *every* single role in your show."

Heidi's giving away our secrets. I *never* should have performed my one-man version of *E.T.* for her, last weekend. But then, she did dangle frosting, straight from the container, as a reward. So? You know.

"He has a photographic mind," Asella says. "For anything. Blocking. Scene work. Bizarre facts that children shouldn't even know."

"He does," Keith calls out from his seat. "The kid knows every musical that ever played this theater. I've never even heard of most of them, and Nate will tell you who, like, the first assistant stage manager of each was."

He's exaggerating. I only memorize the production stage managers.

"I love you," Aunt Heidi whispers, kneeling by my side. She takes my hand and notices my nails. Oh God, she realizes I've got clear polish on.

"All I'm *saying*," is all Asella's saying—now shouting again to mute the cast's roar—"is that you've got two choices: Put the kid on, or cancel the first preview. What kind of ticket sales are we talking here? A hundred thousand?" Nora strokes her mink. "*More*? The damage that's un-calculable? Shall we just write the *Post* headline *for* them?"

"'*E.T.* Go Home,'" the dancer April offers, earning polite applause.

"Or 'Newcomer Saves Show,'" says Calvin. He rubs his stubbly chin and smiles at me.

"Uh, folks?" Roscoe shouts, running into the auditorium from the stage door. Did anyone even see him exit? "Somebody *seriously* needs to handle the press. We've got the *New York Times* in Shubert Alley with a live feed. Nobody can get our publicist on his cell, and they are *quite* literally beating down the door out there. Looking for answers. Or a star."

"Well?" Garret Charles says, slurping his teeth and flaring Gila monster nostrils. He is the oldest person in the room, other than Angry Grandpa, and so I guess he's the senior figure. "What do you have to say for yourself, Nate Foster?"

Asella hops down, landing in a heavy thud, joining every other set of eyes as she turns to me.

And it's only then that I realize my chest is drenched. And that I smell like a . . . *hot* dog.

"Can I change my clothes?"

I stand, dropping the ketchup bottle to the theater floor, a giant squirt covering my heart. Genna gasps.

"Get him to *wardrobe*," Dewey says, shaking purse beads from his hair. They shoot out across the seats, showering the crowd with color.

"*Are we doing this or not?*" Roscoe shouts, now leaning with all his weight—and he's a big dude—into a man in a three-piece suit and a note pad, who's pushed his way into the theater; an old-fashioned reporter with flashing slits where cartoonists usually put eyes.

"We are," Nora says, grabbing Garret by the elbow. "Tell the press—tell *everyone*—that *E.T.: The Musical* will begin previews tonight. As scheduled. No refunds given. No questions asked." She sniffs the air. "No business like show business."

And that's the precise moment when somebody—I may never know who, or whom (I'm terrible at grammar right before Broadway debuts or during Grammar tests)—lifts me up high, higher even than Elliott across the moon, and body-surfs me all the way to wardrobe, past backstage reporters and first-preview floral arrangements. So many flowers line the hallways, you'd think the theater was a funeral home. But no, this is the very opposite of someone dying.

This is someone's dreams coming to life.

Get Me Calvin

(Late afternoon. The day of the first preview.
Aaaaah!)

The room swirls around me.

Mom has one of those hand-held blenders at home, the kind people buy on TV at two in the morning, and that's what my life feels like right now: in the hands of others! The dangerous blades of energy whirring inches from my destiny! Or something.

"Do you want me to get you . . . *food*?" Aunt Heidi says, braiding her own hair in my dressing room mirror, for some reason. "Are you *warm*?"

(Default. Is the child warm?)

"I'm boiling, actually," I say, peeling off my ketchuppy jacket, which I'd never even taken off in the stage managers' office. I wonder if you're still in trouble if you're going on as the star of a musical. Tonight.

I'm going on as the star of the musical tonight.

"Nate?" somebody yells. "Look alive."

"He does this," I hear Heidi explaining. "It looks like he's totally zoned out but really he's off in some vivid fantasyland."

In my defense, Heidi looks the same way when she reads the J.Crew catalog.

Asella slaps me. "Stay with us, kid," she says. "You've got a big evening ahead of you."

"Don't attack my nephew!" Aunt Heidi says.

But I cut in. "Ladies, there isn't time for this." Heidi drops her own braid. "I need everyone out of here for two seconds. I need *Calvin*."

The makeup and wardrobe and stage management people all give in to my demand, clearing the room just as Keith and Hollie are motoring their way in. "Nate, text us if you need *anything*," Hollie says, talking fast and anxious.

Keith butts in: "Donuts . . . Red Bull . . . anything, man."

"Thanks, guys, that could be important. I'll let you know."

They do kind of a weird, solemn bow, like they're at a Japanese funeral or something, and back away into the hallway, with Heidi following on their tails.

"Calvin, to Jordan's dressing room," I hear over the intercom. They don't even use my name. But that's okay. Because hearing Jordan's name? I'm worried about him. I really am.

"Oh! Aunt Heidi," I yell. She pops her head back in, right as Calvin winds the corner, his chest puffing. "I think stage management still has my phone. They took it from me. Because I got in . . . trouble. Sorry."

Heidi's face is a scrumple of confusion.

"Just . . . will you *please* text Libby and tell her the news? She'll want to know."

"On it," she calls out, disappearing into the hall.

"Ladies and gentlemen," from the intercom. *"This is Roscoe. Stay tuned for a bunch of announcements."*

You can hear them chattering. The cast. All the pipes and vents are connected in this theater, and you know what? Everybody's talking about me. Everybody's scared. You could add me to the list.

"Nate, buddy," Calvin says, tapping me on the shoulder, even though I'm already staring at his shirt. (It's a really nice shirt.) "What's happening? How are you feeling?"

Calvin was my savior at the audition. The guy who made everything okay—who gave me my first-ever acting compliment that wasn't from Libby.

"I'm sorta dyin' here, Calvin," I say, fanning myself.

He sits on Jordan's makeup table, folding a clipboard onto his lap.

"So you called me up here, huh? You want to go over blocking, I assume? You want to talk through how scary all this is? How bizarre it is that you're not even *understudying* Elliott"—he looks both ways and drops his voice—"even though you gave by far the most riveting audition, believe me. Nobody else had the balls to slam into the wall, pretending it was a spaceship." He shakes away the image and clasps my shoulder. "So were you just hoping to talk through how overwhelming all this is?"

"Calvin?"

"*Yeah*, buddy?"

"I was just hoping you could get me some deodorant."

He grunts.

"I forgot my Mitchum at home"—the brand he recommended at the audition—"and, well, you know. I was surrounded by girls a minute ago. And didn't want to ask any of them."

Calvin's face breaks into an impression of a face doing a smile. "That's it?"

"That's it, yeah. And maybe a candy bar or something for energy."

"Right," he says, popping to his feet. "Or maybe even something real and nutritious. I'll coordinate with—who was that in the hallway?" He pretends to get casual, glancing at his clipboard.

"My aunt?" I say. If I could redo it I'd go: "My violently single aunt?"

"Sure," he goes, his lips creeping into a smirk. He

pretends to write something on a stack of papers, which is what people do when they try to trick their mood into playing another part.

"My Aunt *Heidi*! She's amazing and full of potential." That's what Mom says about her. But man, that's pretty lame in this setting. Still, Calvin laughs.

"Okay, I'll send a P.A. out to get you deodorant."

"Don't say who it's for!" I say, or maybe yell.

"Relax. Our secret. And more importantly, are you all set on this afternoon's emergency rehearsal schedule, to prep for tonight?"

My ketchup-smeared jacket is laid out on the counter, and I'm clamping Jordan's robe together so tightly at the neck, the thing might weld itself shut. "Gee, I don't think I know anything about today's plan."

Calvin rolls his eyes. "Stage management was *supposed* to visit you, already, but they're probably too busy talking Nora out of killing Dewey."

This makes me laugh on accident.

"Sorry, I shouldn't have said that," Calvin goes, but I can tell he's not sorry at all. "So: You were just fitted for Jordan's costumes, right?"

I think back to Jordan in that zip-up sweatshirt, which couldn't quite cover up his coffee spill. And . . . I think back to the glance I snuck of Jordan with his shirt off.

If only he hadn't mismanaged that carafe, he'd be here now.

"Stay with me, Nate," Calvin says. "Did you just hear what I said?"

"Jordan. Costumes."

"Okay, but I went on. Listen up. Today is all about listening, buddy. *So,* this afternoon, we're going to send you to music for an hour, to run all the songs. And they might lower a few of the keys. You know."

"Since Jordan's voice is still an angel's," I nearly say, "and mine is lower than my Geometry scores."

Roscoe knocks and ducks his head in. "Hey, killer," he says. Not sure if he's kidding here; at any moment I expect him to say I've *actually* caused the death of Jordan. "Calvin, cut the pep talk." Roscoe flips a laundry basket and sits with us. "We've rerouted the afternoon. The crew has agreed to giving you some tech-time onstage."

"*Great,*" Calvin says, clapping his hands together. "This is a *good* thing, Nate."

There is no mass of bullies more intimidating than a Broadway crew. But in a cool way.

"Yippee," I say, clearing a throat that hasn't had a thing to drink today. My lips are so dry, if I smiled they'd probably split. Thank goodness I'm nowhere near smiling.

"We need to run the bike-across-moon sequence,"

Calvin says, checking off a list, "and we need to do the aerial dream ballet with Gertie—"

"Oh my God!" I shout. "I've never been in the harness! I've never flown!"

It's true. There's a whole dream sequence where Elliott and Gertie fly high above the audience, "out to search for their father" in the "great wide canyon of the world." It's superweird, and Jordan always looks like he's going to pee his pants up there.

Which I might just do here. "Um, I'm a teensy bit afraid of heigh—"

"We've *got* to get him up there," Calvin says.

"Yeah, we know," Roscoe says, licking crumbs from his moustache. That thing is like a lunch pail of future rewards. "We're up against a lot here. Nate's never flown. And he's never lifted the E.T. body double out of the ditch. And he's never stood on the desk in the frog sequence—"

"He *has*, actually," I hear, and we all turn to see Garret Charles and Monica, silhouetted in the door frame. "We created the frog sequence *on* Nate. In fact, he created it himself." Garret glides into the room and stops inches away from Roscoe's face (or whatever the British version of inches is). "You're *worrying* the boy."

"I'm taking *the boy* through each step of the day," Roscoe says, standing from the laundry basket.

"Nate," Calvin says, wiping his palms across

a pretty fantastic pair of jeans. "Let me make sure about our errand. We'll get a bag slipped onto your dressing table."

But he lingers, looking like he can't quite leave me with these two goons.

"Thanks, Calvin," I say, giving him the thumbs-up and catching a whiff of myself. Eek.

"Here is the plan for this evening," Garret says, "since it appears the entire company is on different pages." He crosses his arms, turning from Roscoe to begin a slow pace. "Monica is going to walk Nate's track with him, backstage, for the entire show. She'll shadow him."

"What are you *talking* about?" Roscoe says.

"Listen, Roscoe." Garret stops dead, his eyebrows narrowing into keyboard backslashes. "Let's get serious. We all know that *my* team—"

"The dance staff," Monica says, her lipstick growing a shade darker.

"Thank you," Garret says in a "shut-up" kind of way. "The *dance staff* are the only ones who know the true inner workings of this show, Roscoe. Quick changes, exits. Onstage steps and backstage traffic."

"A new musical is the Holland Tunnel at rush hour during a presidential visit," Monica offers, reminding me she's from New Jersey and is thus to be both feared and revered.

"I'd no sooner trust the stage managers to manage the preparations for Nate's debut," Garret says, funneling his voice into a pencil-sharp attack, "than I would with my own dry cleaning."

Here, Roscoe turns a fake-grape purple and offers no argument at all. And then, in a badly timed piece of poetry, Roscoe's assistant Kiana pops her head in, pulls earbuds out, and *actually* says: "Wait! Is it true that Jordan Rylance is *out* tonight?"

Roscoe shoos her away and whimpers slightly.

"Monica will be in the wings to receive Nate, in between each scene," Garret says, with real finality. "We've only time to get him into the emergency sequences today—the bike flight, et cetera, et cetera."

"I have the list of et cetera burned into my brain," Monica says.

(As if I don't!)

"Will we have access to Mackey this afternoon?" Garret asks. "Will Dewey's magnificent casting choice of *Mackey* show up in the next hour, to walk any key sequences with Nate?" Finally, he's letting Roscoe in on the planning. "Or has *Mackey* given up on *rehearsing* altogether?"

Mackey is always claiming that he's only got "one performance in him a day." And that he doesn't like to "waste it on practice." *Real* video game mentality.

"I can check with Mackey's manager," Roscoe says,

pulling out his phone. "But let's not count on anything. Let's . . . let's plan on Asella walking Mackey's role with Nate in rehearsal, today."

(You can't make this stuff up!)

"Nate!" Now Sammy the music assistant dashes in, his toothpick-arms spilling with loose sheet music. "Did you get the new lyric change in Act Two? It just went in yesterday."

"Yes, I—"

But Sammy keeps shouting. Nobody ever takes a kid's word. "So in 'Best Friends For-Never,' we *literally* changed it so that every time Elliott sings the phrase, *'I'm not a scaredy-cat,'* he's now going to sing—"

"I'm no longer scared of that," I say.

"Yeah," Sammy says, his lips racing so fast that the top one almost swallows the bottom. He drops the music to his sides. "Yeah, that's right."

"Nate's on it," Aunt Heidi says, pushing past Sammy. My God, she's back and holding flowers. What a lady. "Believe me, guys, he knows every lyric backward, forward, and loud. Nate, I tried to text Libby, but there's no reception in the theater."

Garret stands. *"Excuse me,* folks. Could the boy have a little *space* in here?" Wow. "Five minutes," he says to Roscoe. "In five minutes, we'll see *you* in the wings, with the full company onstage, ready for Nate's emergency put-in rehearsal."

Roscoe shrinks. God, this is like watching Sondheim get notes from Lloyd Webber.

"We will run the bike sequence," Garret says—for some reason taking the flowers from Heidi and inhaling deeply, as if for inspiration. "After that, we will move on to the E.T. body-double sequence." Here, he massages his jaw and sucks air through some very off-white teeth. "And finally, the finale. And *then* Monica and I are going to have rice and spinach with the boy, and a tea, and take him through a cardio-yoga session. And only *then* will be on our way to our first preview."

But I sort of stopped listening after the letters *F, I, N, A, L,* and *E.*

Oh my God, the finale. I don't have to tap in the finale tonight. Or fake-tap. All I have to do is . . . take the last bow!

"I'd offer some feedback on this *plan*," says Roscoe, "but I have a feeling you're not interested in my opinion, Garret."

"Don't make me say it."

The room clears out, but I watch as Heidi and Calvin lock eyes and make their way to the hall together.

(My work here is done.)

"Oh!" Heidi yells at the last moment, turning back. "About those *flowers*."

Garret hands them back to her and then (seriously) grabs her shoulder and turns her away.

"They're stunning, Aunt Heidi!" They are.

"They were just sitting by the stage door for you," she says.

Garret is now shutting the door in her face. "Flowers are bad luck," he says to Heidi. "Pollen is ruinous in the lungs."

But it doesn't matter, because my heart already took a photo of them.

Those flowers are fancier than anything back home. There's no roses or daffodils or anything people usually throw into an arrangement to glam it up but that just cheap it down. When you're the kid of a flower-shop owner, you learn the tricks. And best of all? There was a single orchid popping its head out at the top, like when Ariel flips her hair in the "Part of Your World" reprise.

"Break a leg, Natey!" Heidi yells, taking the flowers with her and following Calvin (!!!) downstairs. But I manage to swipe the note card that falls from the arrangement. *"Your going to be amazing tonight,"* it says, in Genna's pretty pink writing, *"even if the whole thing makes me sad."*

And then, from the intercom: *"Can we have the full company—and Nate Foster—to the stage."*

"Shall we?" Garret says, reopening the door.

Deep breath. Deep breath.

"We shalleth," I say, tying my robe tight. I slip my

feet into Jordan's slippers and start to follow Monica, but then something stops me. Or everything does. "You're being nice to me," my mouth says.

"Come again?" Garret says, his forehead a knot.

"No, it's just. I sort of thought you guys hated me." We start to walk downstairs. This will be easier to say if I've got the benefit of distraction on my side. "You put me on a diet. Poked me with your cane." My eyes dart to Garret's hand, but he's caneless now. "Cut me from, like, every number."

Monica laughs. "You're not a chorus boy, Nate." We stop on the bend just before the last steps to the stage.

"What my darling and talkative assistant means," Garret says, "is that you aren't particularly useful to a choreographer." He pauses to consider. "You don't know a time step from a toe shoe."

I'm about to protest—I *do* know the difference, intellectually—but Garret holds up his hand before I can speak. The company filters past us, dashing to the stage. To the drama. To slow down and watch my car crash.

"And the *point*, Nate," Garret says, "is that you gave a star audition. A bizarre, freakish, star audition. And this is—I hate to speak in clichés, being British, but—your moment."

And just before we walk onstage together, to a

company of people gathered in a circle, Garret flips me around and bullets his eyes into mine.

"There are people who wait their whole lives to star in a Broadway show."

"And never do," Monica says, putting a hand on Garret's shoulder.

OMG. Of course. Garret never got to be a star. Finally, he knows a way to support me. Lopsided and offbeat. Me. My own kind of makeshift star.

"Go out there for the whole world," Monica says, speaking over a theater full of whispered chitchat. She fake-punches my chin. "No. Go out there for you."

"That's right," Garret says, truly smiling for the first time and ruffling my hair with his hand. "Go out there for you." This must be what affection is. "But try not to get in anyone's way. Or damage any set pieces."

And then the actors begin to clap for me—entrance applause like I'm a TV star and not that kid who cracked on the high note.

And I walk into the center of their circle.

And Genna's blushing. And Asella's smiling—and wearing E.T.'s bodysuit! We finally get to play out all our scenes onstage! And not in a salon!

At least for today. At least for this moment. My moment.

I'd raise my arms and grab my fists and punch the air in a rah-rah victory—like I've seen Anthony do before a big game—but I don't want to kill anyone with my stench. And Calvin's not back with my deodorant yet. So you know what I do?

"We've gotta go out there tonight and show this audience we're ready for the worst of them!"

I talk, is what I do.

And then I catch sight of Dewey in the upstage right corner of the stage, pacing underneath one of his million-dollar video screen sets. It dwarfs him.

"And we've gotta go out there tonight," I say, really shouting now, "and show this audience that . . . that . . ."

Asella steps forward and takes my hand.

"That Dewey has directed," I say, "like, one heck of a show."

And before anyone can whoop or holler, Dewey looks up and nods at me and calls out in a voice tired and raw: "Thank you. Thank you so much, actually. Um. We haven't got a moment to lose, folks. *Get Jake on the bike.*"

And the entire company yells, "Nate!" just as Roscoe throws a harness at me.

"Buckle up, buckeroo—we're sending you to the moon."

Twitter Is Ablaze

(After the show)

They laughed. I know they laughed. That's the only thing I'm certain of.

I'm pretty sure I forgot the lyrics to one part, and just went *"Bum-bum-bum"* for a little while, until the conductor fed the words to me by hollering over the trumpets.

I'm nearly certain that Mackey sweats a lot, because we quick-changed next to each other in the wings tonight before the finale, and the guy was dripping.

And I'm positive that Genna doesn't make eye contact onstage. (I wondered throughout rehearsals if Dewey would ever give her that note—to stop looking at the mirrors and to *start* looking at her other boyfriend, Jordan—but I guess he never got around to it.)

And I guess I'm also sure that to take the final bow—to walk out on two trembling legs that are attached to one body that's finally realizing the hugeness of it all, like getting chosen first for basketball—has left me feeling sick with emotion. Diagnosis: *happysadoverwhelmed*. Treatment: *Uncurable*.

The door pounds itself in.

"Nate Foster!" they scream, crowding around me.

Garret and Monica hold bubbly grape juice. Calvin, my hero, has a clipboard and a grin. And Nora Von Escrow is so done up she looks like a clown. But in a superpretty way.

"Nate, Nate!" they sort of chant in a weird way that nobody commits to.

"Everyone, everyone!" I shout back. "Was I okay?"

(Oh. And I know that Mitchum works. First and foremost. That I put the stuff on three hours ago and I still smell like an atomic daisy.)

"Were you o-*kay*?" Garret says, laughing a hoarse-throated cry.

Roscoe rounds the bend with his team, all of them in black. Kiana has a balloon. "It was all we could find at the last minute," she says, handing me a "Fifty and Fantastic" Mylar happy face.

"Aw, that's okay!" I yell. The whole thing is yells. "I *feel* about fifty years old tonight." I mean that in the sense that my hips hurt so much from the harness.

"You and me both, kid," says one of the grown-ups.

"Do you have notes for me?" I say, gulping from my last swig of pop. "You've always got notes for me."

I'm looking right at Monica, because she's got critiques even when you don't mess up—and I *know* I messed up the waltz tonight, going the wrong way and body-checking Mackey. And also, when Elliott's bike lands in the forest, I hopped out before the E.T. body double was set up, so I knocked over a stagehand. Oh, and also—

"No notes, no notes!" Monica says, looking genuinely embarrassed and sort of fanning her face like we're on a porch. "We're not doing feedback, now, Nate-o. We're *celebrating*."

"Twitter is ablaze," Nora says, scrolling through a smartphone that's twice the size of her heavily armored wrist, which glints with real gems. Nothing like Jordan's mom.

God, I wonder how he is.

"What's it saying, Nor'?" Monica asks. But she looks pretty uninterested in Nora, focused instead—like the rest of them are—on me. Staring like I might at any second disappear. Like my whole performance was that of ghost boy, and they better do their best not to let me slip under the door crack.

"Well," Nora says, reciting from her phone, "one user says '*Greatest musical since* Passion.'"

Roscoe snickers. "Oy."

"And another person—okay, we can skip that," Nora goes.

"What? What!" Monica shouts.

"Oh, *somebody* says our dear Nate is five years too old for Elliott. But you know what I say to that?"

She says a really *terrible* word to that. And hearing such a cuss word come out of a British lady's mouth, you practically expect to see an old bald man behind her, pulling the string.

Speaking of: "Put that away," Garret says to her. "Shall we go to Sardi's? Shall we treat Nate to a bit of a moment?"

"Nate Foster," calls the doorman from my intercom, *"you have visitors at the stage door."*

"Visitors?" I say, standing and suddenly realizing I'm in the robe. It's a pretty awkward thing to be in, with a bunch of adults hanging around. What a lame-looking party, I guess.

"The visitors are just beginning," Roscoe says. "I think we're going to have lines around the block."

"So: Sardi's, shall we?" Garret says, trying to get the group on the same page. On the same *foot*, really. Dance people are all alike, the cattle herders of humans.

"Well," I say, "I have to ask my Aunt Heidi if I can go out."

By now the adult huddle has grown to include Mackey, several of the grown-up chorus, and now Aunt Heidi herself—making, as always, an entrance. Once an actress, always an actress.

"I burst my way through security downstairs!" she says, splitting my crowd in half and attempting to lift me up high. "Good lord," she says, "you've gotten so heavy."

This might be the very worst thing to say to a child actor, who wants to forever remain the exact size and height he is now.

"My *back*!" Heidi says, and drops me, even though she's kidding.

"Bad backs must run in our family," I say, which gets too big a laugh. It's like how everyone's jolly after a really bumpy flight. (Libby says her entire cabin applauded the pilot when they made an emergency landing in Phoenix, once.) God, I wish Libby were here.

"*Well*," Garret goes, putting on his overcoat, "Monica and I are heading to Sardi's. I hope to see you lot there in twenty minutes."

"What about the production meeting?" Roscoe says. "The whole staff is gathering in the house, after the audience clears, to discuss the performance. What went wrong. What we need to change. And where the heck *Dewey's* hiding."

"You people enjoy the production meeting," Garret says, taking Monica by her very thin bicep. "The problem in this show isn't my steps. The choreography will remain the same. Monica and I are off to a very dirty martini."

"Or three," says Monica, batting fake eyelashes.

"And then *somebody*," Garret says, exiting with the speed and terror of thick oatmeal, "can fax my hotel afterward and tell me what we're doing about the *writing* in Act Two."

(Later, I'll ask Heidi if *fax* is an app.)

Mackey breaks in, thank God. "Well, I propose we give the kid a little space." Everyone seems to nod in agreement, even though Aunt Heidi hardly moves. (She's rubbing her back like I'm a buffalo or something, by the way.) And once everyone gets lost, she can't help herself.

"Your parents would just die," she says, dancing around a little. "They would just *die* if they could have seen you tonight."

And suddenly I feel awful for every time I wished they *would* just die. You know when you're little, and you think a bunch of stuff would get solved if the annoying people in your universe would just keel over. I don't think it ever does. I don't think a permanent good-bye is ever a permanent solution to anything. Other than leaving middle school.

"Aw, buddy," Heidi says. "Don't cry. This is a *great* night."

But I can't believe my luck, is all. Or Jordan's luck. His bad luck. Or that Libby is dating a bully back home. That I got laughs tonight. The "with you" not "at you" kind. I can't believe . . . *any* of this.

"I'm not crying," I say, crying, "I'm reacting."

And I can't believe that my dad has been to *every* one of Anthony's soccer, swim, track, and vaulting meets—courtside, ringside, anyside—and he'd never in a million years make a trip to New York. He doesn't trust airplanes, for one. Can't blame him there; they're like toasters with wings, and without the benefit of strudel. But still. And yet.

"I just need a second," I say, pushing Heidi away but in kind of a nice way. "It's just been . . . a *day*."

"Wait'll I text your pal Freckles," she says.

"Wait'll I text my pal Libby!" I yell, but when Aunt Heidi hands my phone back, I don't even have time to scroll for her name, because—

"Quiet that voice," I hear.

The room is so obscured by last-minute flowers and ill-phrased balloons, we can't even see where the voice is coming from. But there she is, peering up from the clutter.

"Quiet that voice and save it," Asella says, shaking her head at me. "I don't think I've ever watched such a gutsy understudy performance."

She laughs to herself, and you can just *see* a whole film play across her mind. Something from her past. Something about an understudy, something funny or sad. Something that I've managed to outfunny and outsad, tonight. Me.

"You must be Asella," Aunt Heidi says.

"You must be proud," she goes. "Proud out of your mind."

"I am," Heidi says. "I don't even have a right to be and I am."

"I'm so excited you're both meeting!" I squeal way too hard. My voice hasn't come back down from the high. No, literally: Half of Jordan's songs were still in the wrong key, and I had to screech them out. Oliver Twist, meet helium. "You're my favorite ladies!"

"What'd I say about protecting that voice?" Asella says.

"Sorry," I say, and then, "sorry" again, and then we all kind of chuckle and I mouth: "Sorry."

"I overheard the production team talking in the house," Asella says, playing with the string of my balloon. And avoiding my eyes.

"Oh?" I lip-synch.

"*Okay*," she goes. "I snuck under a *seat* and *spied* on them in the house."

Aunt Heidi laughs, absentmindedly stealing a Ricola from my dressing tables. (You can have as many cough drops as you want on Broadway and say it's for your voice. Amazing perks.)

"Let's just say they were quite pleased with your performance," Asella says, beaming like a mini-moon. I guess that makes me the earth, which is appropriate; this night meant the freaking world to me.

"You look like you have more news," Aunt Heidi says. Girls can always tell when other girls have secrets.

"All I'm saying," Asella goes, pulling a ski cap on tight, "is that there's rumors our little Nate might be made the matinee Elliott."

"What does that mean?" I say, my voice fraying like wet paper towels.

"It *means* you should keep quiet," both of them go.

Asella takes over: "Because *maybe* you'll get to play this part a couple times a week. Permanently."

I practically die, here. *"Whoa."*

And you know the weirdest part? It would strangely make me sad not to be in the background of the frog dissection scene, because I have a really fun bit with Keith where he picks me up and holds me really tight, like he's protecting me from a berserk frog. But, like, supertight.

"Matinee Elliott," I say, squeezing my robe together.

(But I'd get over it.)

"You wanna join us at Sardi's, Asella?" Aunt Heidi shakes out my dried-ketchup jacket and hands it to me.

"Aw, you kids have fun."

Aunt Heidi chortles and does the whole "oh please" thing—but *God*, does she love being called a kid. She'll probably let me stay up late for a week just in the afterburn of this glorious comment.

"I've got a dog to walk," Asella says, backing up and, if I'm not mistaken, getting a little watery in the pupil region. "You made me practically *bashful* in the wings tonight, Foster. You made the whole company have to step up our game a little." Now her voice is definitely cracking.

"Thank you."

She goes to speak. But she's forgotten her lines. "Blasted theater air," she says, rolling her eyes, pointing at a vent that isn't even blowing. "It . . . gets my throat all dry."

"Me too," I say. "Mine too."

And just when she waves good-bye and curtsies, and just as Heidi turns her back so I can change into my jeans, Asella pivots around again.

"Just keep being you, kid. Whoever that is. Whoever he becomes. Just . . . Nate."

And then she's off, fast as a superhero jackrabbit, disappearing into a teepee of treats and cards, popping down the stairs four at a time. Off to walk Doc.

"So . . ." I say to Aunt Heidi, because otherwise I might cry again. "Sardi's?"

"Sharpie," she says.

"Huh?"

Is this a sick comment on how off-note my singing

was tonight? ("Better to be sharp than flat," according to Libby, "because sharp means you're aiming high.")

"*Sharpie*," Aunt Heidi says again, handing me a fabulous silver pen. "Unused. Bought just for you. For this moment."

Oh.

I want to say, "What for?" To play dumb. To play sweet. Like I haven't dreamed up this exact scenario for just about ever.

"How come?" an old version of me wants to say.

"How many of them are out there?" I say, instead.

"Dozens," she says, her voice tightening, her eyes going oceanic on me. "Maybe hundreds."

"Let's go together," I say, pulling up my jeans, grabbing my jacket. "Behind every good man is, like, an aunt."

We leave for the street, off to sign dozens (maybe hundreds) of autographs.

Whoever I am.

Whoever I become.

Just Nate.

Like If Kindling Could Talk

I'm reviewing the most current version of my autograph in my head, having recently played with one that uses all uppercase cursive letters with a backward slant.

"I know my nice Nikon is in here," Heidi says, rooting through her purse as we get downstairs. "If I can't find it, I'll just use my phone's camera . . ."

And as we pass the stage doorman, who watches sports all day long on this mini-TV, I hear a crispy dry voice calling my name. It's like if kindling could talk.

"Nate."

Coming from one landing down, heading to the basement.

"Over here."

Oh. My. "Um—one sec, Aunt Heidi." God.

"What do you *mean*, one sec?" she says, her hand pressed into the stage door.

I can see a million kids' faces out there, all about my age. On instinct, I look behind me, knowing they're waiting for a star. They're not. Or they are. They're waiting for *me*.

"I just have to . . . say hi to someone."

Heidi cranes her head around, sees him, and gets it. Right off, she gets it, and leaves me, disappearing outside to the crowd. My crowd.

"What are you doing here?" I say, inching toward him. What if he's contagious?

"I couldn't," he says, but then he stops. "It was really hard to be home tonight."

This comes out so honest and real that I almost want to boo-hoo for him. But it's obvious he's done a lot of that himself already.

"Your mom would kill you if she knew you were here."

"Oh, I know," he says, laughing the way you do when something isn't funny at all. "She was pretty conked out on the couch, but I still had to sneak out the fire escape."

"That sounds incredibly dangerous," I say, even though I've hung out on a few myself. "Wait—they've got fire escapes at hotels? I thought you were staying somewhere fancy."

He checks the knot on his scarf.

"We were. We were in a so-called fancy hotel at first,

just so we could put the address down on the company contact sheet." He licks his lips. "But we found some studio apartment on Craigslist. For Mom and me."

I mentally correct it to *For Mom and I*, and *then* congratulate myself for not correcting him out loud, and *then* realize he's actually right. Grammar isn't my thing, but I think you know that.

"So what are you doing here?" I say. "You should be home, getting better."

"Oh, *really*?" he says, cocking an eyebrow so hard, his left ear practically wiggles. "Because you seemed pretty happy to be up there tonight."

"You *saw*?" I yell.

"Hey, boys?" This, from the doorman. "We gotta close up backstage in a few minutes. You guys gotta get on your way."

I don't really "get" doormen. All they do is sit around watching football and flirting with the chorus girls. Actually, wait. I *do* get doormen. They're like every uncle who ever *didn't* lift me up high to play Superboy. It's like my whole life, everyone's been afraid of getting too close to me.

"Yeah," Jordan says, "I saw the show."

We ignore the doorman altogether, because if there's one thing about doormen, they never get up from their chairs.

"I can't believe this." I really can't.

"I was home," he says. "And my mom drew me a bath . . ."

Instantly, he's embarrassed.

"Funny term, right?" I say, to save him. "It's like—don't draw me a bath. I can't sit in a cartoon."

He laughs. It's a pretty funny joke and I thought of it pretty fast.

"But I had to see the show," he says. "I had to see what it looked like. It was amazing."

He sniffs a big gob of something back into his throat. His eyes water. Is he emotional or just sick? Or both? Or are my eyes wet, and am I watching this whole thing from underwater?

"I'm not infected or sick or anything," he whispers. "The doctor says I just lost my voice from too much practicing. Go figure."

"I'm so embarrassed you saw me play you tonight," I say.

"Boys, I'm serious," the doorman says. "I'll call security." But the guy's bluffing. There is no security. *He's* security.

"I made up half the lyrics to 'Whitest Boy on Earth.'"

Jordan giggles the way rich kids do, with extra consonants. "Those were some pretty original lyrics, yeah. But I preferred *'Bum-bum-bum'* to half the stuff they've got me singing anyway."

We both smile, but I think for different reasons. I don't even know what I mean but I'm sure I'm right.

"Or half the stuff they have *Elliott* singing," he says. A paper bag crinkles and I realize he's holding a big something. "Or half the stuff they've got *you* singing," he says, quieter.

"Oh please, Jordan. This is so your role. You're so Elliott. Have you seen the front of the theater?" His name is as big as a Volkswagen Golf, which Anthony's first girlfriend drives, by the way.

"Yeah, well . . . anyway," he says. I bet he doesn't even know what a Volkswagen is. I bet his dad drives a Porsche. Or drove one, once. "You did a really good job, Nate."

"Thanks."

"I'm going to count to three." Oh man. Eddie's standing over us now. Apparently doormen *do* get up from their chairs, if two sensitive boys are having a heart-to-heart.

"Just have to get something from my dressing room, Eddie," Jordan says, switching to Prince Boy mode. God, the kid's a good actor. "My inhaler. You know. Asthma."

Jordan fakes a cough, which is pretty hilarious since he's managing a real one.

I follow Jordan up the stairs. I wonder if I smell like ketchup. "This is really crazy," I say when we arrive in his dressing room.

"Yo, kid"—Eddie, over the intercom—*"your aunt's at the stage door and she's looking for you."*

"We gotta make this quick, Jordan. Get your inhaler and then we're outta here."

"I don't have an inhaler," he says, handing me the bag. "I don't have asthma."

I peer into the bag. *"Pierogies?"* Pierogies. Huh. The spectacular carb delicacy from our hometown. "You brought me . . . pierogies."

"Yeah. Yep."

Pierogies are like ravioli except filled with potatoes and fried with onions. So just imagine that for a second: It's like somebody was like, "No, the *bread* part of the pasta isn't enough. How do we put another starch into it?" They're not even allowed to teach pierogies in nutrition class, because the minute a kid learns about them, they never eat anything else ever again.

"What are these for?" I say. "These are so random."

"They're from *Pittsburgh*," Jordan goes. He looks superwhite.

"Well, duh. Yeah."

"Just like the Penguins. And the Pirates."

These are reportedly Pittsburgh sports teams.

"Well, I'll make sure to share these with my aunt." I scrunch the bag closed. "She loves hometown food, even though she pretends it's for hicks."

"You don't get it, do you?" Jordan says. His hands shake.

"Get what? I almost never get anything, so."

Jordan slumps into his makeup chair. Or tries to. I'm so much taller than he is (shocker!), and his chair was adjusted for my height tonight; Jordan misses on the first try and crashes pretty hard to the floor. But he's one of those kids who doesn't find normal stuff amusing, so he doesn't laugh and neither do I.

"The *Penguins*," he goes. "The *Pirates*."

Oh God. Am I supposed to come up with the next clue in the list? I'm terrible at these games. Plus, I've got fans waiting outside.

"*P*-words?" I say.

"*Nate?*" I hear from the floor below Jordan's. "What's going on? This is ridiculous."

Heidi's voice sounds more mad than confused at this point. Almost nothing can get her back from this state, unless anybody's got spare brown sugar Pop-Tarts sitting around.

"I gotta run, Jordan," I say. "It was amazing of you to, like, congratulate me though."

"Nate, I gave you the gifts."

"What?"

"The penguin drawing. The pirate bear. The Heinz ketchup. *Things from Pittsburgh, like us*."

What?

"The *orchid*?" I kind of yell.

"What *about* orchids," Heidi says, pushing her

way into the dressing room. "Oh. Oh, hi."

"Hi," Jordan says, not even looking up. Man, he looks depressed. Like how I feel when the Tonys are preempted by a shooting in the Hill District or something.

"Where's your *mother*?" (She actually says this to Jordan.)

"She's at home, probably thinking I'm taking the longest bath ever," Jordan says. Now he laughs to himself. Okay, I guess he finds some normal stuff amusing, because I'm laughing too.

"Do you need me to call her?" Heidi says. Good for her for just sort of *running* with all this. I'm as baffled as she is and trying to piece together this new revelation.

Jordan's the gift giver?

"Don't bother calling her," Jordan says. "We're subletting around the corner. I can run home in two seconds."

"You look terrible," she says.

"You sound like my publicist," he says. "Mom made me Skype with him tonight. They're trying to get a human interest piece placed in the Village *Voice* about how shows should cancel their first previews when the star can't go on."

"Nobody reads the Village *Voice*," Heidi says, without thinking. That's when I realize she's roping me close. Holding me just like in *E.T.* when he's cooped up in the metal death chamber.

"Yeah," Jordan says. "And who cares even if anyone *did* read that paper? They shouldn't cancel previews just 'cause somebody can't go on. Not when the understudy is as good as Nate."

He's not even talking to us, he's speaking into the floor. I'd never noticed the carpet. It's a weird off-brown that reminds me of my pierogies. My stomach groans.

"Let's get to Sardi's, buddy," Heidi says. "You must be starving."

But I've stopped staring at the mysterious carpet and started staring at the mysterious Jordan.

"We're closing the theater in two minutes," Eddie's voice booms out.

"Let's *go*, boys," Heidi says. "After you, Nate."

But it's funny, because she runs ahead first. And then Jordan and I take a bunch of heartbeats to follow her out. And when Heidi pops into the ladies' room on floor two, that's when I have my chance.

"You gave me those gifts? They weren't from Genna?"

"Genna?" Jordan says, blast-laughing. His tongue is yellow with cough drops.

"Um," I go, like an idiot.

"No. No, Nate. I mean, I had her leave you the first note. For me. But . . . she's chasing Keith, now. After I kind of turned her down flat."

Keith!

"The orchid?" is all I can say in return.

"I Googled your mom's flower shop."

"She doesn't have a Web site."

"Yeah. It took some research."

Heidi's washing her hands. The sinks in the theater are a million years old, and they all splat water like hyperactive geysers. This should buy us another minute in the hallway, because she'll have to mop up her blouse with one-ply paper towels. In fact, you can hear her swearing pretty bad right now.

"But eventually I found a story your brother Anthony wrote online," Jordan says. "In the school paper. About his workout regimen . . . or whatever—"

No *whatever. Regimen* is exactly the word Anthony would have used.

"—where he'd lift weights near your mom's orchids. In your garage."

Jordan's eyes brighten with each revelation, like I might be truly freaked out that he's a stalker. I am. But it's also wonderful.

"I haven't made a single friend in New York," he blurts. "You were—you, like, *are*—the only person I could relate to."

"Please, Jordan. You're famous. And mean. And rich."

"I'm not. And only kind of. And are you *kidding* me?"

"Let's go," Heidi says, shouldering her way out of the bathroom.

But somehow she sees that we're talking about something. Something real. Her face changes; you can actually see the little muscles make up their minds to switch around.

"*Three* minutes," she says. "And then I meet you outside the stage door." She's off.

"All I'm saying—" Jordan goes.

"I thought you hated me."

"My mom hates you."

"Great."

"No—wait," he says. "I mean, she called you the 'confident and clueless type.' Which she claims is more dangerous than 'jaded and experienced.' She wanted me to, like, intimidate you." He rolls his eyes at this. "This whole thing . . . she set me up to take you down, Nate."

"Um . . . is this supposed to be a confession?"

"No, it's *supposed* to be . . . all I'm saying is that I sort of watched you in rehearsal. When I wasn't front and center. And I thought we might be . . . maybe . . . the same." He waves it off. "I secretly hoped we could be friends or something."

"You sent me a pirate bear so that we could be friends?"

"To be fair, my mom thought I was giving that

to Dewey. Same with the orchids. Which are really expensive."

"You didn't even sign the cards."

"I didn't want you to think it was *weird*," he goes, struggling hard past a lumpy throat that's probably one-part scratchy and one-part feelings.

"It *was* weird, though," I say.

He bites his lip. "I didn't want you to think I was . . . you know."

Oh.

I scrunch up my face in a really over-the-top bad actor way, to show that I couldn't possibly know what he's referring to. But I want him to say it, so bad. I want somebody else like me to say it.

"I didn't want you to tell other *people*," he goes. "Especially, like, if my mom found out. She'd go on and on about how a real leading man has to behave like . . . a real man."

"Oh."

He looks like he's going to cry. He looks like he's crying. He's crying. He's bawling.

"Oh my God, Jordan. I don't—" I look down to find my words in the linoleum stairs. "Look, it's actually really nice, what you did."

The lights from three floors up shut off, clinking to darkness from a circuit breaker somewhere. Must be Eddie.

"The penguin drawing? It's up on my aunt's fridge."

The hallways above get darker, darker, humming quieter one by one.

"And the pirate bear? Honestly? I've slept with it. I *sleep* with it. Because my aunt doesn't have good heat in her building."

"At least we've got heat in Pittsburgh," Jordan goes. We both laugh. I'm still looking away. It's like too much truth all at once.

"And the orchid? It was really pretty, even though Garret didn't allow it in my dressing room. In your dressing room." I look up now. "I'm not even allowed to be *near* my mom's orchids. She has names for them. Somebody asked her once, totally as a joke, if she liked her orchids more than her children—"

Now the hallway is totally purple, darker than black. The only light peeks from around the stairwell, Eddie's little TV, with our eyes adjusting in the bug-lamp blue.

"—and my mom goes, 'I don't like to pick favorites,'" I say. "She literally said that. About choosing between orchids. And me."

"Nate?" Jordan says. It's the smallest sound.

"Yeah?"

But I barely get to the *Y* of the *Yeah* before Jordan's brushing something soft and warm, like the inside of a bagel, across my lips.

And then I feel a boiled breath all over my cheeks. An exhale. And I'm sweet and sour and hot and cold all at the same moment. An ice cube doused in diesel.

"Oh wow," Jordan says. He's far away now, backed into the wall. "Was that—I'm sorry."

Doused in diesel and lit on fire.

"I didn't," I say. Because I didn't. "I don't," I say. Because I don't.

"Me either," he goes.

"I've never had—I've never done that."

"Me either," he goes.

I have, actually.

I did it to Libby. With Libby? But not for real. Not for real because it didn't mean what this meant. It wasn't actual. It was like when you have Sweet'n Low instead of sugar. But then afterward it's bitter.

"Whoa."

It's not bitter now. It's weird and different and foreign and disorganized. It's not bitter. It's incredible.

"Let's get out of here," one of us says.

There's a thing, a true thing we learned about in Spanish, where people can wake up after a traumatic head injury and suddenly speak another language. Word for word. In perfect sentences. Languages from countries the person's never even *heard* of. That's this.

I want to stand on a roof in Jankburg and go: "Look! I didn't get struck by lightning."

I want to tell everyone.

"We shouldn't—" I start.

"—tell *anyone*," Jordan says, completing my sentence.

Except, no. "Oh. I was actually going to say that we shouldn't kiss by the stairs. In case we lose our footing."

And then: happy adult voices, suddenly. *"So we'll start at the top of two, and work through."* Loud ones too.

We grab the railing and hang our heads over, watching the production staff passing Eddie, on their way to meet Garret and Monica for filthy martinis, or whatever they're called.

Dewey follows last, even after the P.A.'s and the assistant lighting designer and a janitor. He looks like he was left totally out of the discussion after the show.

"Dewey!" I call, letting my face catch in the cast-off TV light. He stops.

"Who is that?"

"Troublemakers," Eddie says, turning down the game and putting on a big camouflage coat. We gotta get out of here. I bet Eddie hunts kids in his off-hours.

"It's Nate," I say, stepping into the little glow. Dewey shields his face to see me.

"Oh," he says. "Wow. Hey." He looks so tired. So

broken by what should be, like, the best night of his life.

"I didn't see you after the show," I say. "And I . . . um . . . I just wanted to say thank you."

"For what?" he says, laughing. "According to everyone, *E.T.* is a hit in spite of my worst efforts."

"I heard it was amazing tonight, actually," I say.

"Oh yeah?" Dewey goes. "Stay off the Internet. Believe me. You can lose an entire month reading your reviews on Amazon."

"No, not the Internet," I go. "I don't have a smartphone."

Dewey laughs again. "Maybe I'll get you one for opening night. I haven't decided on the cast gift yet. I was *just* told I should have given out first *preview* cards tonight. But apparently I'm the last to know everything about etiquette." Here, he sort of picks his nose.

"All I'm saying," I say, loud enough for it to travel backward, "is that somebody really cool saw the show, and told me in person how amazing it was. Even the video parts. All of your parts. Your vision."

Dewey takes a big breath. "That's nice, Nate. Thank you." He pulls out his phone. "Here, I'm sending your info to my assistant."

"Calvin?" (Please, *Calvin* knows my name. Calvin is my secret weapon!)

"No, my assistant from the world in which I actually know what I'm talking about," Dewey says. "He's in California. He'll hook you up with a new smart-phone. For free."

Come to think of it, Jordan's got a pretty old phone too. "Make it two," I say.

Dewey grunts. "Should I get you a tea while I'm at it?"

"Nah," I go, channeling Libby's timing. "Who do you think I am? Garret?"

Jordan laughs in the dark.

"Who is that? Is somebody else up there?"

I don't know what to say—does Jordan want to be seen? So I just get quiet.

"Too long of a day," Dewey says, shaking his head. "Get some sleep. You're on again tomorrow night. Oh—and we're stealing the bit where you almost kneed E.T. in the nuts. We'll make sure to teach that to Jordan."

He shuffles away into the cold outside.

And you know what? Those fans are still out there. Because you can hear them sigh in unison. Sighing that he's not me, I just know it. They don't even real-ize he's the director.

"I'm sorry you had to hear that," I say to Jordan.

"What? About kneeing E.T.? It was hilarious. I was going to steal it anyway."

"Ha," I say. "Let's get out of here."

"You go first," Jordan says. "I'll hide behind you

and run home." He wraps his ears into the scarf, and looks like a little pierogi.

Eddie hacks up a lung and flips off the TV.

"*Friggin' kids.*"

The blue around us is gone, replaced with an emergency exit red.

"I'm locking up," Eddie announces to nobody at all.

"Jordan?"

"Yeah?" he goes.

"I don't think we should feel bad about it." In fact—"I'm going to tell my best friend."

He doesn't say anything, so I just say it again: "I'm going to tell Libby we did that. She'll be cool."

Jordan steps forward, and it scares me, his face flickering a cast-off crimson. "Okay?" he says. And then: "Okay," again—and this time he means it.

And we rush past Eddie, before he can draw his rifle and hunt the two of us. Just Nate. Just Jordan.

Just two normal boys, fleeing their stage door in one vacuum-packed *whoosh*, greeted by an army of girls—and a couple boys—all screaming their brains out. Somebody takes an iPhone photo, and then everyone does, and Aunt Heidi has *somehow* found an upended crate and is standing in the back of the crowd, documenting the whole scene on her Nikon. I guess she found it after all.

And somebody yells NATE!

And somebody yells ELLIOTT!

And I couldn't have done any of this tonight if I hadn't been cut from every number, and sat out on the sidelines, and studied Jordan doing it all before I had to. *Got* to.

And just when he ducks out to run home, I grab his scarf and spin him back to me, and I toss the pierogies to Aunt Heidi, and I hand Jordan the silver Sharpie.

"You sign first."

What Just Happened

"Are *you* playing Elliott now?" a girl asks (I think).

"Can you sign underneath your photo?" another one does (I think).

"Will you take a picture with us?" a boy says (I think).

It's hard to keep up with. It's fantastic. It's disorienting. I'm mostly thinking about What Just Happened. About Jordan running ahead after signing just one program, escaping into the alley, back to his Mommy. No—to his mom.

I wonder what's he's thinking right now. If he's as nervous—as hyped up—as I am.

"Did you replace Jordan?" somebody calls out, and that finally breaks my spell.

"No!" I shout. I must be really screaming, because a mother pulls her daughter back, and another kid starts to cry even, I think. "No, Jordan's really awesome. You all have to come back and see him in the show!"

"I already have tickets to four performances in March," says a girl in a *Spring Awakening* hat. She is holding an actual house cat, swear to God.

"Cool," I go, shivering.

Heidi is snapping pictures, and I'm trying to greet everyone who stuck around so long for me, but my Sharpie hand is cramping. No matter. I hate writing longform but will make exceptions for autographs.

"Do you have a fan page!" a girl hollers.

A fan page. I don't. Not anything like that.

"Nope, ma'am," I manage.

The girl is probably nine, but I call her ma'am. It's just that I don't have a fan page and so it kind of knocks me over, the question.

In fact, last year somebody created a Nate Fagster page on Facebook. Believe it or not, a hundred people Liked it in the first twenty minutes, and then Libby and I filed a complaint with Facebook and they took it down.

But still, somebody in my grade took a screen shot of that hate-page, where somebody else had uploaded the photo of my very worst school portrait. My eyes were blinking. I wore an unstrategic striped shirt that made me look a million pounds. My world-famous underbite was sticking out as far as it possibly could, making even the photographer recoil in horror.

And so even after the Nate Fagster page was taken down, people spread that photo around, and it went kind of mini-viral. Like a cough that never becomes a total infection but still keeps you home.

Libby pulled me aside in the cafeteria and showed me the photo on her iPhone, because everyone in the world has an iPhone, except for me and Jordan and Anthony (who has a *Droid* and might be getting an iPad). "You're not going to like this, Natey," Libby said.

She was right. I not liked it so much that I not went to class the rest of the day.

Mom didn't understand. "It's just a photo, it's not even real. It's on a Web page site." She said all of this while bathing her little dog, Tippy, in our kitchen sink. She never cleans the sink out afterward, by the way—which is why, so often, our dinner salads smell like wet mutt. Not that we have salad that often. Not that we eat as a family.

"Well, we're going to make a fan page for you!" a girl squeals. I must look her dead in the eye in a way she's never been looked at before, because her friends giggle, and she sort of turns in on herself.

"Pick a good photo," I say. "Please pick a nice photo."

If you Google-Image my name you find exactly

three pictures. The famous school portrait, which I call Fagster-the-End-of-the-World-Photo. A pretty okay one where Libby and I got Jankburg press coverage for the time we went door-to-door, collecting money for a Carol Channing Museum we were cooking up. And a picture of a guy named Nathan Jackson Foster, in Poughkeepsie, who whittles presidents' faces into frozen Brie. So, yeah.

"Were you asking for it?" my dad asked that night, when he overheard me and Mom talking in the kitchen. "Did you do something to provoke those harmless boys into making a mean thing about you?"

I remember, distinctly, that he was eating a left-over Primanti Bros sandwich, its hundred layers splaying forth on his lap and falling into couch cushions. Pittsburgh is the only place in the world where you'd put french fries *inside* a sandwich. (I'm adding this in the *plus* category for Pittsburgh, by the way.)

"No, Dad," I said, with Mom scooting me out of the kitchen, because I was getting Tippy riled up. "I wasn't asking for it. You don't *ask* people to create a *Web page* about you where they call you every name under the sun."

"It'll give you character," Dad said, turning up *Jeopardy*. He never knows a single answer, but don't remind him. "Stay out of those boys' way."

"Do you have a girlfriend?" someone asks, and

then Heidi the Protector's next to me, grabbing the Sharpie and capping it.

"Come on, buddy."

My hands are practically blue, they're so cold; ever since getting the news that I was going on as Elliott, I never quite got anything to eat, and the enormity of this night is hitting me like a Mac truck. (I'd love to be a Mac-truck driver, just transporting makeup from theater to theater, sea to shining sea.) Point is, I think the endorphins are finally wearing off, here. I've never been a kid who got runner's high—that's Anthony's territory. Me? I suffer from runner's low. *My* highest moments come from singing in the woods with Feather. Or during the nights of sleep where James Madison and the Bills of Rights aren't making nightmare appearances, taunting me. Torturing me. Calling me a fag.

"Do you have a girlfriend?" a brazen girl calls out again.

Aunt Heidi pulls my hat down tight over my ears. "Let's get to Sardi's," she says.

"Who's Libby?"

That stops me.

"Who's *Libby*?" I say. They know Libby?

"Yeah," says the brazen girl, she of Pippi pigtails and dangerous eyes.

"Your *bio*," the girl says, reading from it: *"For Libby: I hope you were right about me."*

"Oh, *Libby*."

It warms me up, just saying her name. It spreads white to my blue hands and nourishments to my belly. As if by just reciting the word *Libby*—my best friend, my coach, the person who kind of knew me before I knew myself, because girls grow up so much faster— is enough to give me, like, vital nutrients.

"Libby is my best friend. Ever. And if you liked anything I did up there tonight, basically she's responsible for rewiring my every bad instinct as an actor."

"What does it *mean*?" the redhead says. She's just about the last of them standing here, clumped with a troupe of dancer girls, all wearing the same shiny blue jackets. Miss Judy's Center for Theater Arts. "What does *I hope you were right about me* mean, in your bio?"

"It means . . ." I start to explain.

But then I wonder what it means too. I wrote it at the last minute, in the car ride with Mom to New York. Libby never even approved the bio, too busy sleeping that last night away with me. Our legs intertwined, our hands all over each other. Nate Foster: the least threatening boy in America.

"Come *on*, Natey," Heidi says. "Gotta get there before they close. Get you a hot drink." She's smiling in this weird way, like she's distracted all of a sudden.

"It means I hoped I lived up to Libby's expectations. It means I hope I'm as good as she swore I was back in her basement. It just means I hope that . . . Libby was right."

And that's when a scorched alto voice says its most important dialogue yet.

"I was," the Voice says, creeping up from behind my shoulder like a fire alarm—but the good kind. The kind that takes your whole class out to the school parking lot for half of a test.

"I was *definitely* right about you, Natey-greaty."

And *that* is when I faint.

Fade-out

The worst part, I suppose, is the humiliation.

"At least you didn't hit your head."

It's not the fact that I split my lip open.

"At least you didn't fall into anyone."

It's the fainting-in-front-of-my-new-and-only-fans part.

"If you hadn't taken *forever*, we'd have waited in Sardi's like your aunt instructed. But we got worried. And curious."

"I guess the rule going forward is that maybe you shouldn't sneak up on me. But thank you. For being worried."

Heidi brings out a tray of hummus and carrots.

"I thought we'd have a nice healthy snack to welcome our guests," she says, popping around the apartment and throwing things into closets.

"You guys planned *all* of this out *today*?" I say.

"Of course," Libby says. "What did you think? I'd drive to New York at the very last moment to see you in the *chorus*?"

Libby's mom gives me a squeeze and makes her way into Freckles's old room, and Heidi hits the lights in the kitchen and heads to the bathroom to wash her face. This'll take an hour or three, because she cried so much, earlier tonight, that she had to keep reapplying greasier and thicker makeup. She kind of actually *looked* like E.T. when she got to my dressing room.

"So," I say.

"So," Libby goes.

"Was I awful?"

She launches Heidi's only throw pillow at me. "Listen, rock star," Libby says, bypassing the hummus altogether and taking the plate right back to the kitchen. "You were perfect. Just talk faster. Once you know the lines better."

Libby Jones always cuts to the chase.

I hear Aunt Heidi's phone dinging in the bathroom a bunch of times, and then she kind of giggles. It actually sounds like she's whinnying into a *hand* towel or something.

"Everything cool in there, Aunt Heid?"

She cracks open the door. Her cheeks are red—even through a shocking amount of green foam.

"*Apparently* we are seeing a late movie with that *Calvin* next weekend," she says, sighing and giggling some more and then shutting the door.

Go, Calvin! I bet he'll even buy our tickets, because he's that kind of guy. Wow.

"Speaking of *lucky*," I start to go, frustrated tonight's rhythm with Libby feels a little off. But then—

"I thought you'd never ask," Libby says, pulling the rabbit foot from her backpack.

"How did you know I was going to ask where it is?"

"Please, Nate. I knew how you were going to *bow* tonight," she says. This makes sense. She *taught* me how to bow. My instinct at the end of our basement shows was always to wave or curtsy. "*And* I knew you'd be grinning from ear to ear that you got to replace *Jordan*, of all people."

She tosses me the foot.

"Oh, yeah, Jordan," I say. My stomach and heart switch roles. "Yeah, him."

"Yeah, *him*," she says, laughing, scrunching her face, kicking me a little. "The kid we hate, right?"

"Nah," I go, quicker than I mean to. "I mean, he can be a little bit of a twerp, but . . ."

"A *little* bit?" she goes, grunting hard enough, now, that Heidi swizzles her head back out to check on us. She's moved on to a blue facial-foam layer and is looking pretty sea-creaturey.

"Nate, saying Jordan is a little bit of a twerp is like saying *Gypsy* is a little bit of a star vehicle."

I kick her back. "We had a turning point," I say. "Jordan and I turned over a new leaf."

"You're purple right now. Do you know that? You are the color purple."

"Brilliant movie," I say. "*Great* book."

"Iffy musical," she interrupts—but doesn't change the subject. "You look like an *eggplant*."

"What's with you and all these vegetables? It's disconcerting."

"What's with you and all these big new words? It's discombobulating."

Heidi gets a tip-toed glass of water from the kitchen. This is hilarious because there's already a glass in the bathroom. Eighty bucks she's checking on us to make sure we haven't started a fire or traded drugs or something.

"Anyway," I go.

"Well, maybe Jordan's grown up," Libby goes, swinging her legs down and kind of picking at an afghan thread. "I know *I've* changed a little."

"You mean not wearing mismatched socks?"

"You noticed?"

"Libby, for God's sake. It's one of your chief

qualities. *You* not having mismatched socks is like *me* having a magically healed underbite. And—"

"Are you and Jordan more than friends?"

She says it so quietly, it actually gives me a believable excuse to say, "What?" Heidi's back in the bathroom again, thank God.

"Are you—" Libby stops and looks at me and then looks away and then looks at me again. "Are you guys, like . . . more than friends. Or something."

I hate being known this well. For my whole relationship with Libby, being known this well has been the selling point. The riddle on the Popsicle stick.

"I don't," I start. "No. *Know*, I mean."

"Well, that sort of says it all." She gets up and roots around inside her luggage, but there's nothing in there. She's stalling. Libby never stalls. She blurts.

"Are you going to change on me?" she finally says, looking up with tears in her eyes. I've never realized how legit pretty they are.

"No!" I say. "No, I'm the *same*. I'm just the exact same."

"Okay," she says. "So you're not going to be all different and secretive or anything?"

"Libby!" I ricochet my eyes over to the bathroom, but at least Aunt Heidi's got the water on full blast. No way she can hear us. "I thought our generation was supposed to be the one that didn't care about, you know, what people are. Or aren't."

"Our generation isn't you and me," she says, ker-plopping into the futon and then hugging that throw pillow, hard. "Our generation isn't stuck in Jankburg, alone." She takes off her glasses and rubs an eye.

"Please, Libby. You've got Billy O'Keefe."

"Bill," she says, "and I don't. I—I broke up with him. Turns out he wasn't at all into the Gay-Straight Alliance thing . . . so I wasn't at all into the *him* thing. Or something."

I want to shout, *"Oh my God, no way!!!"* but figure it's best to play it cool, so I just go: "Oh my God, no way."

"Way."

"Well, *see*? That sounds more like our generation already."

She lightning-bolts the glasses back on and turns right to me. "Our generation didn't promise each other to get married if they were both thirty and hadn't met somebody."

"Come on, Libby, we're thirteen. Not thirty. We've got . . . like . . . a *really* long time to figure all that out."

"You are so terrible at math," she says.

"What?"

"You literally couldn't have done that math if you'd wanted to. Thirty minus thirteen." But she's not saying it meanly. There's a smirk on her tongue.

"Whatever," I say, laughing. She's right. The only counting I've mastered goes five, six, seven, eight. I reach over and hug her, which is pretty awkward, because we're getting older and stuff, but it's also the right thing to do. Heidi would approve.

"There's been nobody like you, Natey." Libby kind of laughs. "Not Bill." She laughs harder. "Not the other girls, that's for sure. The so-called lucky rabbit foot is false advertisement."

"Well, there's nobody like you here, either, Libby." I hate how it comes out, because I really mean it, but it sounds like I'm just saying that because she did.

"You're just saying that," she goes. But she knows I mean it. Please, she knew how I was going to *bow* before I did. "So . . . Jordan hasn't replaced me?"

Only in that a kiss with him felt like a real kiss, I want to say. But I just go, "No way. Not even close. Three Jordans is like . . . one Libby."

"Thanks?" she asks, her forehead suddenly littered with dubious eyebrows.

"You're *welcome*," I say. Give Libby an inch and she'll still refuse to run a mile in gym.

"You should call your mom and dad," she says, and Heidi somehow hears *that*—did she overhear *all* of this?—and opens the bathroom door. "And rub it in their faces, Natey. Tell them you became so much more famous than Anthony tonight."

Dad told me to come back a star. Dad will flip when he finds out how much extra money I made this week for playing Elliott.

"You *should*, Natey," Heidi says, toweling her squeaky face. Uh-oh, it's a night she's got her retainer in. I hope Libby doesn't snort. "They're going to— well, I don't know *what* they're going to say, because your mom still hasn't called me back yet tonight. But you should phone home right now!" She starts to hand me her cell.

"No," I say. "In the morning. It's so late. I don't want to wake up Dad and Anthony. They'll be up in a few hours to do weights in the garage." Right by Jordan's meticulously researched orchids.

Heidi does a whole "suit yourself" routine, hugging me good night and telling me how proud she is. How I'm the greatest Foster alive, and she never could've pulled off what I did tonight. "Thanks, Aunt Heidi." And I just let her have the moment. I don't even downplay it or discount it. "Thank you, thank you."

And Libby and I flip off the last night.

And settle into the terrible slats of the futon.

And it's like there's nothing except everything to talk about.

"I don't want to tell them anything tonight," I

finally say, when the honking and occasional drunk voices from the street get to be both too quiet and too loud. "I don't want to share any of this with Mom and Dad. Or Anthony."

"Not even Feather?" Libby says. "You dog would be very proud of you. Especially since you've played so many scenes opposite him in *my* basement."

"Nah," I say, smiling, trying to find a good spot on the pillow. "He's not so hot on the phone."

"Why don't you want to spill your news?" Libby goes. "It's, like, the biggest news ever."

"Because if I tell the family Foster I went on as Elliott, they'll ask what that means."

"Right."

"And then they'll ask if I'm getting more money."

"Right."

"And then they'll say, Why didn't you just get the part in the first place?"

"Totally."

A radio blares from a passing car, and I close my eyes.

"And then they'll ask if Jordan's jealous of me, and Dad will follow the wrong story line and ask if there's something we can do to get rid of Jordan."

Libby laughs.

"And then Anthony'll be all, That's cool. Does that mean you're not coming home for a while officially, and can we turn your bedroom into a steam room or something for postgame detoxes?"

Libby laughs really hard now, but she's getting heavy with sleep.

"And then Mom'll take the phone back and say, Serves those people right, from the other side of town, for thinking they can just have *everything*. A big house with a carousel, and a mom in fur coats all day long, and a kid starring on Broadway."

"Your mom'd have a point," Libby says, yawning.

"Except they don't have all those things. Jordan's dad is . . . never mind."

"What?"

"Jordan's family maybe isn't as well off as you'd think."

"Ah, I see," Libby says, rolling over to face the other way. She'll flip back in two seconds, though, because the most annoying street lamp is on her side of the futon.

"You see?" I say. "What do you see?"

She rolls back over. Told you. "You've got secrets now with Jordan. You're protecting him."

But I ignore her there.

"And since I promised Jordan to *keep* his secret, I wouldn't be able to tell my mom that *his* dad lost his job. That they were almost bankrupt before Jordan got Elliott."

I open my eyes and look up at Heidi's ceiling, which is so dark I could fall into it forever.

"And I wouldn't be able to tell my dad that Jordan's like me, too, and that families who live in bigger houses aren't always happy. And that starring on Broadway can actually be a lot of pressure."

Here, my voice gets cracky. Darn theater air, huh, Asella?

"Uh-huh," Libby goes.

"And I definitely wouldn't be able to tell my brother—or anyone—that Jordan and I kissed tonight."

A hundred thousand seconds go by in one, and then Libby puts her hand on my shoulder and just sort of doesn't say anything, because sometimes that's the best way to say it all.

"And that's that. And that's maybe why I'm not going to tell my parents—yet—that I became a Broadway star tonight."

Libby pulls her hand away and we close our eyes and we're both about to fall asleep, when I add one more thing.

"It actually doesn't even matter to me that I missed the whole party at Sardi's because I fainted and scuffed my knee."

"Those pants needed to go anyway," Libby says like a dream. Or in a dream. Or singing out from a dream.

"All that matters is that I'm proud of myself."

Tonight I lived up to me. Not Dad or Mom, or Anthony's legacy. Tonight I was myself, because everybody else was taken. "For literally *once* I'm proud of myself."

It's superquiet, and the sirens all shut off like in some weird cooperation, and Heidi's done in the bathroom, and Libby's mom is snoring the contented moans of somebody doing better than the doctors could have even imagined.

Tonight was for me. Nobody else's opinion matters. Nothing else matters but my being okay with that.

And . . . we're . . .

Asleep.

And then from nowhere, Libby: "You wanna go on Twitter and see what they're saying about you?"

"You bet your freaking life."

"Yay!" Libby says, bolting upright and typing my name.

I let the rabbit foot drop behind a cushion for probably a million lifetimes. Who needs a dead animal's foot when you've got the luck of your own racing heart?

"Loading, loading," Libby says, shaking her phone.

And we sit arm in arm, legs intertwined, and stare into her iPhone (because everyone has an iPhone except for me), and we wait for *Nate Foster* to turn up some results on Twitter.

"Here's one," she says.

And I don't even care what they're going to say, because Libby and I are back to normal again, even if everything else is different.

"Eh," I say, flicking to the next Tweet, "I've been called worse."

Because as long as I've got my best friend—as long as one thing stays the same—everything else can change in a kiss or a curtain call.

Oh, One Last Thing.
No Big Deal

"hey u up?"

"whos this"

"um its jordan. i got ur # on the contact sheet."

"oh hi jordan! yeah im up couldnt sleep tonight"

"me too."

":)"

"☺"

"oooh your phone does fancy emoticons"

"haha. yeah. so . . . my mom killed me when i got home bc i snuck out."

"i was just gonna ask about that"

"yeah but its ok it was worth it."

":)"

"☺ so anyways . . ."

"hey . . . my aunt heidi and calvin are seeing a movie this weekend and we should go with them? i'm already invited i bet calvin would pay for ur ticket too" "oh i'm sort of grounded now. excpt when im at the show ☹"

"oh no"

"yeah."

"sorry jordan"

"but maybe we could like watch a movie on my laptop sometime at the theater. like on a matinee day between shows or something?"

"ok!"

"or whatever."

"sounds fun :) <<< pretend thats a fancy emoticon"

"haha ok natey."

"hey any ideas what movie we should watch?"

"we can figure that out whenever bc i have net-flix streaming we can watch like a zillion movies whenever."

"awesome!"

"yeah ☺ night nate."

"night jordan. oh btw have u ever seen something called 'whatever happened to babe jane'?"

"haha no whats that is it for babies?"

"mayb im not sure. heard its really funny and important though"

"ok cool ill see if netflix has it hey i should go before my mother finds me awake."

"oh alright cool"

"hey nate?"

"yup"

"i like u. or whatever ☺"

"hey jordan i like u or whatever too. insert fancy emoticon here"

"haha ur funny."

"thanx"

"if theater doesnt work out u should consider standup comdy. thats a compliment."

"haha ok"

"srsly nate i need u to teach me how to nail elliott's jokes sometime."

"ok but then u have to teach me how to not crack on the high note in act 2 sometime"

"its a deal."

"its a deal"

"it's a . . . date i meant."

"me too"

"ok then. c u soon nate."

"c u soon jordan"

"☺☺☺☺☺"

"well now ur just showing off :)"

Acknowledgments

Thank you to the entire cast and crew at Simon & Schuster Books for Young Readers—especially Navah Wolfe and David Gale—for all you do.

Thank you to the booksellers and educators and authors and librarians—and kids!—I've met since the publication of *Better Nate Than Ever*. Also, thank you to my friends, both online and off, for putting up with the breathless self-promotion of a debut novelist.

Thank you to my boyfriend, Brian, for being my boyfriend, Brian.

Thank you to Karen Katz for always pointing out the offensive jokes in my first drafts.

Thank you to my family—especially my dad, for paying for all those theater classes, and my mom, for driving me to them.

Thank you to Brenda Bowen for being so Brenda Bowen-ish (Google her).

And thank you, *you*, for being the kind of person who chooses to read books. I'm grateful!